# THE ALMOST ONE

## THE ESCORT SERIES VOLUME 5

### N.O. ONE

# THE ALMOST ONE

# Warning / Foreword

**Before you continue...**

**The Almost One is the fifth volume of a series of six.**

It is graphic and morally on the fence, containing extremely sensitive material that may not be adapted to your needs. If you need specific details of things involved, please visit our website for a list of warnings.

www.author-no-one.com

If you're okay with all of this, just remember... we warned you.

On the plus side, the lead female is strong and proud and these men come with a fire extinguisher.

If you're still reading after all of that then, by all means, sit down, relax, and enjoy the filthy, bumpy road ahead.

To reiterate:

***!! If you have triggers, please do not continue. This is not the series for you. !!***

Seriously, if you don't want all the angst and smut with some suspenseful darkness thrown in for good measure, stop reading.

To you...

The women of the world, fighting for your basic human
rights.

The LGBTQ community, fighting for your lives.

We see you.

We support you.

We stand and fight beside you.

# CHAPTER ONE
## RIVER

*I* *have nothing...* nothing.

Depressing as this thought is, I'm struggling not to break out into song. Everything is fucking fucked and I can't do a thing about it.

When did my life become so out of control that I'm in this position...?

In an ex-client's home—one who happens to be my husband, a mafia boss, *and* the man who has been an immovable rock in the storm that is my life.

"You didn't have to burn my fucking apartment down to make me stay here, you know, Marco." My hands are on my hips and a smirk is playing on my lips as I stand in front of his desk, watching him watching me, his hands steepled under his chin.

"I'll buy you a new one, *Tesoro*." He raises a brow and narrows his eyes, waiting for my next move.

The last few days, he's been great at keeping me from wandering into the dark depths of my own mind. And as much as I want to follow the path to my self-pitying destruction, Marco won't allow me to do that. Which infuriates the Hell out of me, mainly because he's not wrong, but also because I've never been that girl; the one who combusts at the first sign of trouble or difficulty. I'm the girl who gets back up again, who moves forward, no matter what.

It's going to take some time to get back to being that girl, but this determined man in front of me won't let me fail. *Asshole.*

"No. I'll take a look at some listings this afternoon, maybe I'll find something closer to Hell's Kitchen." I match his raised brow, knowing full well I will be looking at fuck all, but it's fun to tease him.

As much as I've been living in the shadows, he's been right there with me. He's been spending every moment he's not with me in here, his office, working harder than any man I've ever known.

Finding out which member of the team Enzo called in for clean-up in my apartment will tell us who the one to burn it down had been, but it's proving to be difficult.

Apparently, it wasn't in their briefing because it draws attention that Marco doesn't want.

*No shit, Sherlock.*

Having the police turn up at my brother's home almost had me confessing to everything, and when they told me my apartment was practically ashes, I thought that was it. The moment my life would completely crumble. But then I looked around me, at the faces of everyone I love, and I knew I had to keep going.

Now though, it's my turn to ease the mind of this man in front of me. To give him something to keep *him* going. The circles under his eyes have been getting darker, and I know it's because of the nightmares that keep me from finding peaceful sleep.

"Are you teasing me, Tesoro?" The devious smirk on his pink lips widens and he moves his hands behind his head, leaning back in his lush leather chair. The way the black material of his button-down shirt tightens around his biceps sends a jolt of pleasure straight through me, but I try not to tense up, knowing the surprise I have in store for him.

"Well now you've gone and ruined it." Folding my arms over my chest, I fake-pout. "Well, fuckedy fucking fuck, asshole."

That ought to do it...

"Oh, Tesoro." Marco rises from his chair, palms flat on the desk in front of him, eyes full of desire. "Are you *trying* to make me punish that sweet ass of yours?"

"Oh, no, I would never..." Moving close to the desk, I pick up the pen he was just using and drop it on the floor. "Whoops." Like I'm acting out a cheesy porn film, I slowly turn and bend to pick it up. The short, skater-style red dress I'm wearing barely covers my ass, so as I bend down, I'm giving him a full view of everything I know he wants... with a little extra surprise.

I hear a sharp intake of breath, followed by a low growl as Marco moves so quickly, I'm barely standing before he's behind me. Pushing down on my back to hold me in my bent position, he strokes over the globes of my ass and down my bare crack.

"This is new." As he reaches the toy I bought today, I almost combust at the pleasure running up my spine when he gently tugs at it. His fingers continue their journey to my pussy, no doubt feeling the wetness beginning to drip down my legs. "You're so fucking wet. I'm not going to waste a fucking drop."

I've never needed to lube up with this man, it's like he has a direct link to my cunt and he's never letting go.

My eyes almost roll into the back of my head and I groan when Marco drops to his knees and licks me from ankle to apex, where he sucks my clit into his mouth. His nose nudges at the new butt-plug, causing all kinds of sensations to spark over every inch of my body. He still has one palm on my lower back, holding me in position while the other slowly creeps up my thigh, his fingers following the same path as his tongue did moments before.

"Fucking delicious." Two fingers find their way inside me, and oh, holy motherfucking Jesus, that feels so good.

"Fuck, Marco."

*Slap!*

Once, twice on my right ass cheek, sending vibrations through the butt-plug and no doubt leaving a red hand-print. A handprint he is now gently soothing away as he rubs slow circles into the sting before spanking me once more.

With the combination of his fingers inside my pussy, his mouth on my clit, and the butt-plug in my ass, I'm not surprised my building orgasm is on the brink of exploding as he reddens my flesh.

"Oh, God." I can't help the gasp that escapes my lips.

"Not God, but close enough. Come all over my tongue, Tesoro. Let me drink you down."

Taking my clit between his teeth, he continues to assault my senses, the low rumble of his voice sending me over the edge, and I come with a scream. "Yes!"

He doesn't stop and the next orgasm is so close it almost hurts.

"Again."

Holy shit. *Yes!*

And I do. But this time, it leaves my legs feeling like jelly and I'm not sure I can hold myself in this position any longer. I'm surprised I've lasted this long, to be honest.

"I can't get enough of the way you taste."

With a final lick over my sensitive clit, he removes his fingers, gliding them over my slit and ass, circling the butt-plug before reaching around to my stomach. I'm still bent over, so the friction from the material of his pants against my bare skin is a heady feeling as he towers behind me. Pulling me up to standing, my back against his front, his breath tickles my neck.

"You're so fucking sexy, Tesoro." His lips press against the skin behind my ear, and he palms one of my breasts, squeezing gently and pinching the nipple between his finger and thumb.

"You're not so bad yourself, Mr. Mancini." Turning to face him, I wrap my arms around his neck, peering up into those steel-gray orbs. Though he may look tired, the way his eyes crinkle at the corner when he smiles makes everything else around me fall away.

There's just something about Marco Mancini that has me second guessing what I thought I wanted. Remembering Polly's words about discovering the other half of your soul—words I admittedly laughed off at the time—I find myself obsessed with this man in my arms. But at the same time, I'm wary. This may feel different, more intense, than the love I thought I held for Kai, my Eros, but I'm not sure I can trust it. The traumas I've experienced in this last year could drive anyone crazy, so maybe that's what has me questioning myself.

Whatever it is, I'm going with my gut for once, because my mind is fifty shades of fucked up right now.

The artificial light reflects in Marco's eyes as they dance between mine, and I push aside my warring thoughts to take him all in. His hair is a little longer than usual, the ends curling ever so slightly now, and he hasn't shaved in days, but every version of him sets my senses on fire and has my clit tingling at just the thought of him being near me.

"Did you get this for me?" He taps at the butt-plug in my ass, causing an aftershock to ripple up my spine.

"I mean, I got it for me, but we can clean it up and use it on you if you want…"

His eyes widen as he strokes his hands up and down my back, before a glint of mischief appears and he smiles.

"Never tried it, but with you, Tesoro, I'll try anything once."

It's my turn to be in shock, but I think I hide it well, the corners of my mouth rising higher.

"Well… Okay th—"

He doesn't let me finish, pressing his lips to mine softly at first before coaxing my mouth open with his tongue and slipping it inside. There is no fight for dominance, just the gentle caress of flesh against flesh as one of his hands fists into the back of my hair and he growls into my mouth.

It doesn't take long before the kiss turns almost feral, like we can't get enough of each other, and within moments, he cups his hands under my ass and lifts me. Wrapping my legs around his waist, my bare pussy rubs against his clothed body.

That won't do.

"Off." I tug at his shirt impatiently. He knows what I want.

"Fuck." In the next breath, I'm standing, watching as the gorgeous man in front of me unbuttons his shirt quicker than the Flash, ripping it off and throwing it onto the floor before unzipping his pants and stalking back over to me.

I run a finger over the prominent *V* of the last word scripted on his ribs. It's all in Italian so I have no idea what it means. I want to continue my exploration of his body, dipping my fingers into the ridges of his chest and feeling every hard inch of him, but I hold off as he reaches for me. He grabs the bottom of my short dress, pulling it up and over my head, growling once more when he sees that my panties aren't the only undergarment missing; I have no bra on either.

"Exquisite."

"You going to just stand there?"

His devilish grin returns as he grabs me by the ass again and I wrap my legs back around him, my bare pussy against his bare skin.

Leaning my head forward, I take his bottom lip between my teeth and tug gently before devouring him. Our tongues slide over each other, teeth nipping, lips sucking, and I find myself rubbing against him, the friction from the sexy trail of hair below his belly button almost turning me into putty in his arms.

Marco walks us to the closed door of his office and slams my back against it, holding me in place as he lines up his cock with my pussy while still completely owning my mouth. The wall is cold against my skin, but it's soothing at the same time.

He slams into me, the small sting as he enters mixed with the pleasure is fucking beautiful, and I tilt my head to the side to give him better access to my neck as his lips trail their way across from mine. With one hand still gripping me, and the other practically gouging holes into the door behind me, Marco fucks me with abandon. It's fast, it's rough, and it's full of passion—just like everything he does.

Rolling his hips, he slams into me, again and again, and another orgasm begins to grow. The sensations flow through my rock-hard nipples, my fingertips, every nerve ending, as our heavy breaths and the slapping sounds of our bodies fill the room.

"Oh, holy motherfucking shit!" I scream as the orgasm hits, my pussy pulsing in time with my pounding heart when the hand Marco is holding me up with pulls out the butt-plug.

One, two, three more hard thrusts, and Marco grunts out his own release as I continue to pulse around him.

"I'll let that one go, Tesoro. I love that filthy mouth when I'm pounding your perfect little cunt." The smirk he gives me before claiming my lips once more almost melts me. If I *could* melt any more than I currently am.

Is there such a thing as an orgasm coma?

I think I'm about to find out.

When he finally relents, pulling away from me, he slides his cock from me and guides my legs gently back down to the floor. I have to lean against the door to hold myself up; jelly legs are a real problem.

"Put this on. I'm taking my wife upstairs." He throws me his black shirt, which only just covers everything, as he slides his pants back on, hiding away his still-hard cock. The man has stamina.

"Your wife's a lucky woman." Buttoning up the shirt, I step toward him with a smirk.

Rounding his desk, Marco opens a drawer and pulls out a folded cloth, coming back toward me and falling to his knees again, all the while keeping eye contact with me as he brings the cloth up my thigh from my ankle, cleaning away any remnants of our cum.

"I do love a man on his knees. Maybe I should get you a cushion for next time? Do you like pink?"

He shakes his head in amusement, as if he doesn't know what to do with me, before he stands, grabbing my legs as he does, and throws me over his shoulder like a mother-fucking caveman.

*I love it.*

"Come on, Wife." He lightly taps my ass before opening the office door and heading toward the staircase.

Halfway up the stairs, the sound of Stefano loudly clearing his throat stops Marco in his shirtless tracks.

"Sir, you have a visitor."

"Tell them to fuck off, Stefano. I'm busy." He begins to move up the stairs again, only to pause as the sultry tones of a woman interrupt our ascent.

"*Buona sera, Marco. Sono venuta in un brutto momento?*"

I really need to learn Italian, because this bitch sounds like sex on a stick with that accent and it pisses me off. I'm not usually one to hate on other women for no reason, but this one already has my hackles rising.

"Yes, it's a bad fucking ti—" Marco's words end abruptly just as he turns around.

They obviously know each other and I can't figure out what's bothering me more... how perfectly put together this woman looks, or the fact my husband is suddenly speechless at the sight of her while half-naked with me tossed over his shoulder.

I move to slide down from my position, placing my bare feet on the stairs beside him, and turn to look at our intruder.

In any case, it's undeniable that she's fucking stunning. And nope... not today, Satan. The way she looks at me—like shit on her shoe—makes me want to punch her in the tit. Then she averts her gaze to Marco, trailing her eyes all over his naked torso.

"Marco, who the fuck is that? Who the fuck are you?" I'm addressing them both at the same time, my eyes burning holes into anything they land on, my neck beginning to ache with how much I'm swinging it back and forth.

Usually, I wouldn't be this... overprotective? Yeah, that's what I'm calling it. There's just something about the way she looks at us that doesn't sit right.

Slowly, she smiles like a cat who knows her mouse is trapped in her claws, using a finger to push a strand of her red hair behind her ear before speaking. Looking Marco head on, she proudly announces her identity.

"I'm his fiancé."

# Chapter Two
## Marco

Fucking hell. Are all the women in my life trying to kill me?

"Elizabeth. It's nice to see you, but now is not a good time." I can feel River's blood boiling to the point she just might burn my house down, but I have to tread carefully here.

Elizabeth Ambrosio is not just anyone.

She's the only daughter of the most powerful family in Naples. Disrespecting her would be a sure way to start a transatlantic war. Nobody has time for that shit.

"I've just arrived from the airport, I thought I'd come directly to you." With her arms crossed at her wrist and resting on her lower stomach, where she holds her clutch, she's the picture-perfect display of grace and class. Born and bred to be a wife in my world, she knows how business is done and how important the role of a queen is to a mafia king. She's perfect in every way.

Except, she's not River and never will be.

"Let me introduce you to my wife, River." At my words, my Tesoro raises her chin and proves her mouth is just a little bit faster than her brain.

"And wife trumps fiancé." She doesn't say it, but the word "bitch" is just begging to be heard.

Enzo chooses this second to jog into the living room from the kitchen. He quickly takes in the situation before promptly turning on his heel and walking right back to where he came from. Fucking coward. Useless right-hand man he turned out to be.

Placing my palm at the small of River's back, I love the fact that her body naturally sways toward mine. She probably doesn't even know it's happening and would deny it with her last breath, but I know it and that's all that matters.

"Elizabeth and I were never formally engaged. Our families did all the planning." My voice is firm, my tone leaving no room for arguments.

"It is the way of our world, Marco."

I had once believed that as well. That said, it doesn't matter. My union with River is solid on all fronts and my wife has something Elizabeth never did... my love.

Getting the message that Elizabeth isn't planning on leaving until she's said her piece, I turn to River, my hand clutching the back of her head as I bring her mouth to mine in a heated, necessary, kiss. One that sends a clear message, and I'm grateful that River knows this game all too well. The ass slap is just an added touch to drive the message home.

"Go upstairs and be ready for me." My whispered words, however, are not for show. They are a promise.

"Don't be long, *husband*. I'm not the waiting kind." I let the corner of my mouth tick up in amusement at her muttered words, shaking my head when the volume of her next ones are loud enough for the whole fucking house to hear.

"I've only had two orgasms today. You're slacking on your duties." *Christ.* "Also, you need to get dressed. I don't share." This time, she aims her warning at Elizabeth, who is as unmoving as always, as she shrugs off my shirt and hands it to me. I don't have time to scold her for walking around naked as she bolts up the stairs and disappears from view.

Without a word, I lead the way to my office, sliding my shirt back on and making sure my slacks are buttoned as well.

"What is so urgent that I have to take precious time away from my wife?" Elizabeth and I never actually had anything physical. All the arrangements were set up by our families and, at the time, I had no idea River would be in the picture, so Elizabeth was as good a choice as any.

"I didn't realize you were still together."

As I sit behind my mahogany desk I see her reaching for the door, presumably to close it.

"Leave the door open." I may have loved the little jealousy act River played out there, but I refuse to give her any reason to think I'm not one hundred percent committed to her and our marriage.

"It is a private matter, Marco." I swear, this woman's voice barely fluctuates, even when she's not happy.

"Leave it open or walk away. Your choice."

She only hesitates for a second before, with a barely perceptible sigh, she makes her way to the chair across the desk from me and sits like a royal on her throne. I don't want a war, but it's becoming increasingly difficult to hide my annoyance.

"Now, what can I do for you, Elizabeth?" With my elbow on the armrest, I place the side of my face in the nook between my thumb and index finger. I'm already bored with this conversation and it's barely even started.

Knowing River is upstairs, naked and waiting for me to ravage every inch of her body, is seriously pissing me off with every second that I'm wasting.

"Like I said, I was told you were no longer together." I take a second before answering, watching her and trying to get a clear feel of her angle. On the outside, she's completely put together. Long red hair parted in the middle and curling in just above her breasts. Her lips perfectly made with her signature burgundy lipstick, and cheekbones that have made more than one supermodel jealous. But just beneath the surface, I can discern the aggravation. It's clear her family has sent her here to get the job done.

*The job* being... me.

"Who is your source?" I could force it out of her but, really, I don't give enough of a fuck.

"Oh, Marco. We don't need to discuss names, it's unbecoming." Translation: the "who" is a possible threat.

"As you saw for yourself, we are most definitely still married and if you hadn't interrupted us, we'd be fucking right now." My crude language is intentional, I need to see her reaction to better assess the situation.

Not a flinch. Not a gasp. Not even an eye roll, which would have been completely out of character.

"There's no need to be so common, Marco. I understand that men have needs, but this is bigger than your little infatuation. Both chapters of our organizations are counting on our alliance to stay strong and in control. This"—she rolls her hand in the air like she's gesturing to something inconsequential behind her, or someone—"obstacle is not boding well for either of our families."

Linking my fingers together, I lean back in my chair and stare at Elizabeth until I can sense her discomfort.

"I am married and by law of our traditions, there is no dissolving our union. So I'm not sure why you're even here, to be honest." Our vows were promised in blood, there's no going back from that. But more than that... I refuse to let River go.

"There is one way." Her words are muttered but I hear them loud and clear. It takes every ounce of my tightly-reined-in control to hold myself back from throwing Elizabeth out of my office and my home.

"Watch yourself. Those are words that can start a war you cannot win." On the outside, I'm the definition of calm. On the inside, I'm consumed by my rage.

"Hmm, she knows nothing of our protocols. She's unpredictable and hot tempered. What happens when she can't handle her duties? What happens when she's the cause of bloodshed in the streets of our cities? What will you do then, Marco?"

I don't need to explain myself or my actions. I am the underboss, second only to my father, as the ruler of our families. More often than not, I put some humanity in my job, but when veiled threats are aimed at my wife, all fucking bets are off.

Standing, I place both palms on the unforgiving wood of my desk and lean in as close as I can so Elizabeth can see the determination in my eyes. So she can see there is no changing my mind. Ever.

"We're done here."

Only when Elizabeth has been cordially escorted out of my home does my mind focus on what's important.

Taking out my phone, I decide it's time to play a little with my food.

**Me:** Are you naked on our bed?

**Tesoro:** No

She's such a little liar.

**Me:** Are your legs spread wide enough for me to see your cunt?

**Tesoro:** You wish.

I don't just wish; I know she's up there naked and ready because this thing between us is too strong to resist.

**Me:** Now, play with your clit and get yourself nice and wet for me.

**Tesoro:** *middle finger emojis*

Because she can't see me, I let my grin spread wide across my face. There are five middle fingers on that text message. Which means I get to punish her five times.

Sometimes, it's just too easy to rile her up and it's never *not* fun.

Leaving my shirt draped over the back of my office chair, I turn off all the lights and slowly make my way up to our bedroom. I'm teasing myself by taking my time. Torturing is more like it but just like my wife, I'm a fan of the antic-ipation. The chase. The expectancy of seeing her laid out on my bed, primed for the taking. Barefoot with only half of my zipper pulled up to avoid losing my slacks, I reach my door and push it all the way open with only my index finger.

Just as I knew she would be, River Fox-Mancini is propped up by the pile of pillows at the headboard, not a single stitch on her. Long, silky legs are an open invitation to my watering mouth, and right there, at the apex of her perfect thighs, are two long fingers circling her swollen nub.

"Such a good girl." I try to keep my tone even, but my libido is running wild like an out-of-control forest fire, making my voice crack on the last word. I don't need to look at her face to know she's enjoying my fight for control.

"It's not for you, it's for me. I happen to like getting myself off." I don't doubt her and, more than that, I love how comfortable she is with her sexuality.

"Was stripping in front of the help and our guest part of your own personal foreplay?" I push my slacks down and palm my cock. My strokes are nearly painful as I watch her fingers accelerate her practiced movements. Without consciously doing so, I realize I'm jacking myself off to the rhythm she's set for herself. Or maybe she's flicking her clit to the beat of my hand. In the end, it doesn't matter. The only thing I care about is making my wife feel good, and for that, she needs to know who's in control.

"Maybe. I didn't hear you kick our *guest* to the curb." The word "guest" is spit out like venom and the way she's overtly showing me her jealousy is making me harder by the second.

"I have manners, Tesoro. Unlike my wife, who not only bared her ass to a woman she didn't know, but also made our staff uncomfortable." Stefano didn't see a fucking thing or else his eyes would be frying like eggs in a pan. Elizabeth? Well, I suppose she got a good eyeful of a perfect ass. "Not to mention you flipped me off not once..." I kneel at the altar of my wife's cunt without missing a beat of my strokes, "but five times." With my free hand I reach out and pinch her nipple—hard—before grabbing her entire tit and squeezing until I can hear her breath catching in her throat.

Still, she defies me.

"You were being a controlling asshole, so I figured I'd let you know."

"Hmm, that's six. Are you feeling a little neglected, Tesoro?" My eyes scan the length of her body as I decide how I want to punish her.

"No. I'm pissed off."

Change of plans. I jump off the bed, releasing my cock and making my way to the dresser, where I slide out a thick leather belt.

This will do nicely.

"Don't stop playing with your clit, Tesoro, you're going to need the distraction." Folding the belt in two, I snap the leather together and glance over my shoulder as the sound echoes around the room. River cocks a beautiful brow at me as though to say, "Is that all you've got?" and I can't help the roar of laughter that erupts from my mouth.

This fucking woman.

"I'm not afraid of being tied to the headboard, Marco. Actually, I'm a little disappointed that's all you've got."

She's right about one thing, I'm about to bind her wrists. Not because I want to scare her, but because not being able to touch me has always been punishment for her. If she ever tried to keep me from running my hands all over her I'd probably lose my fucking mind, so it's something I can understand.

Taking her wrists, I wrap the belt around them three times before I'm confident she's incapable of getting loose, then I secure her to the steel hook I had installed during her rebellious stage, during which she slept elsewhere than her bed.

My bed.

Our fucking marital bed.

"How am I supposed to rub my clit now?" That fucking mouth is going to be too busy to sass off.

The belt I slide from my belt loops, I use on her ass.

At the foot of the bed, I grab on to her ankles and in one quick move, she's turned onto her stomach, the perfect globes of her ass in the air for my viewing pleasure.

"This ass, Tesoro?" One flick of the wrist and the sound of leather against flesh makes my cock jump with a familiar thrill. "It's mine. Mine to punish and mine to fuck."

The red flash of skin is immediate and now I can't think of anything except fucking it.

But I've got a sassy wife who needs me.

In rapid successions, I decorate her ass cheeks with streaks of pinks and reds until I reach a total of six.

Six lashes for six disrespectful words.

Only then do I turn her right back around and discard my belt as my eyes fall to her rapidly rising and falling chest. When I look down to her pussy, I almost come all over myself at the sight of her wetness coating her lips and thighs.

"Is it even a punishment?" I'm talking to myself, but of course my wife answers.

"Not even a little bit."

With her arms angled back and her tits on show, I straddle her chest and grab her jaw, my fingers digging into her flesh until she relents and opens that delectable mouth of hers.

"To the back of your throat, Tesoro. Less talk, more sucking." Then I push my aching cock as far back as it'll go, my balls slapping against her chin with every thrust. Our eyes are fixed on one another, her nostrils working overtime while her lips and tongue do a fucking fantastic job of getting me off.

"I rather like you jealous, Tesoro. You spend so much time pretending not to care that I have to admit, this is refreshing." I push my dick so far down her throat I can hear her gagging, see her saliva gathering at the corners of her mouth. "Do you actually think I could ever leave you for another woman?" I pull out slowly, giving her the impression that I'm waiting for an answer, but instead, I push right back inside the hot cave that is currently making my balls ache with need. "You are mine, River. You have been mine since the first time I laid eyes on you. Fuck, even back then you were the most beautiful woman I'd ever seen in my life. You were always meant to be mine."

Her brows are pinched; I can tell she's trying to figure out what the fuck I'm talking about. And goddammit, I want to tell her everything.

Maybe I should. Nathaniel is no longer a threat. Maybe, like this, she'll be too busy to kick my ass.

Pulling out abruptly, I slide down her body and lean in to whisper my vow against her lips. "But more than anything, River Fox-Mancini... I am yours. In this lifetime and every other that follows."

Just as my tongue breaches her open mouth, I slide my cock between her pussy lips. Somehow, we manage to fuck and make love all at once.

We grunt and sigh, cry out our pleasure with *yeses* and *fucks*. We bite and kiss and I bruise her perfect skin with my fingers and teeth.

I mark her body the way she's marked my soul until we're both too tired to ask unnecessary questions.

# CHAPTER THREE
## RIVER

"Any messages for me, Sheryl?"

Much to Marco's dismay, the wide-leg pant-suit has become a bit of a staple in my new wardrobe, and as I breeze into the office space, I stop in my tracks at the sight in front of me.

Both Sheryl and Lily are wearing similar dresses in a royal blue color. Exactly the same as the color of my suit. We all stare at each other for a beat before laughing stupidly hard. We look like we all called each other the night before to check what we're wearing today, or like some kind of girl band getting ready to do a press tour.

It's one of those moments that wouldn't raise a smile from someone who's not here, but for us, it's just another reason I love my job.

"Oh, man. This shit's funny. Like, did you guys really not know?" Lily finishes stirring cream into her coffee by the machine and glides back to her desk. She's not in the office as much as Sheryl, but we agreed to make sure she had a comfortable desk space she could customize for when she's here.

"Nope. No clue, but considering this is the third time in the last two months that we've all matched, I think it should become a thing." I laugh as soon as I've spoken, clearly joking, but it is stupidly funny.

"I think this is the second most colorful thing I own, so unless you want to spend most of your time in black…" Sheryl chuckles as she clutches at the coffee in her hands, her elbows resting on her desk.

"Nah, I'm good." I wink. We both know my wardrobe choices are wilder than the average New Yorker.

"To answer your earlier question, there are no messages. But I do have information…" Sheryl wags her brows, a clear sign she knows something she's been dying to tell me. "Brandy finally told that client she was seeing to fuck off."

"Good for her. I still want to see her for our meeting next week though. Can you remind her about our lunch, please?"

"Already did, boss lady. Fresh coffee pot is ready in your office too. You need to get some more sleep, babe. It's beginning to show."

From a random person—like a certain annoying Italian woman I can think of—this would be insulting, but Sheryl is nothing if not brutally honest. I know she's not saying it to be a bitch, she's looking out for me, the same as I would for her.

"I know, I haven't been sleeping well. I'll get there. Thanks for the coffee, Sheryl. I'm gonna go and squirrel away in there for a few hours. Get all this fun paperwork done."

"Don't forget to take breaks from the screen," Sheryl calls as I walk into my office, and I smile. She's like the office mother hen, even though it's mostly just the two of us up here.

Closing the door behind me, I take a deep breath, inhaling the citrus scent from the diffuser on the bookshelf. It's so strong it fills the room, and I love it every time I step in this space. My space. Citrus is supposed to calm work stress and help improve concentration, which is perfect. Petal would be proud.

My new office chair is amazing. I replaced Polly's old one for this luxurious gray swivel chair. The cushioning is perfection and it molds to me every time I sit down, engulfing me and accepting me as one of its own. A girl's gotta be comfortable while she's working. This chair and the photo frame on my desk holding a picture of Ev, Petal, Kai, and me from a few years ago are the only additions I've made so far.

I'll eventually make this place completely my own, but I've had other things on my mind. *Surprisingly.*

The letter tray has several unopened items lying there, ready for my attention, so I get to work opening them and dealing with them one by one. Transferring all of the licenses for the club into my name is taking its sweet ass time, but Rome wasn't built in a day and all that.

A small, bright red envelope with no postmark catches my attention. My immediate thought is that it's from Marco. Fuck knows why, it's not like he's a regular at sending me love notes in red envelopes, but I wouldn't put it past him. The envelope isn't sealed so, with a smile, I pull out the white card. There's a single red rose on a thorny stem in the center on one side and I flip it to see what's written on the other.

*Do you miss me?*

Okay, so that's kind of sweet. It doesn't say it's specifically from Marco, he hasn't signed it, but who else could it be from?

The intercom buzzes and I lean over to press the button. "Everything okay, Sheryl?" She loves using this thing, it's her new favorite toy since she installed it for me a few weeks ago. She said it's much better than the old, crackly version Polly used to have.

"Yeah, you've got a visitor. And I haven't decided if you're the luckiest woman in the world or hiring a new stripper for ladies' night."

Who the fuck...?

"Who is it, Sheryl? I'm kind of busy today."

"Says he's your best friend and he's got lunch."

Kai? What the fuck is he doing here?

"Okay, send him in. Thanks Sheryl."

The intercom buzzes off as the door to my office flies open, and in comes Kai in all his construction glory. I laugh, thinking back to how Sheryl described him, and it couldn't be more true. His hair is long enough to be in a topknot now, and his beard has grown out to about an inch long. It could do with a little grooming, but it's Kai. He could always do with a little grooming.

He's wearing a high-vis vest over a black T-shirt and his work pants with a million pockets. The steel-toed boots are dusty and leaving marks on my carpet, but I'm having the floors redone soon so I let it slide.

"Thought I'd drop by and see the new place, Miss Big Boss Woman. And I bought some bagels." He holds up the bag in his hand, a seemingly-carefree grin on his face like all our troubles never existed.

"While I love that you've brought bagels, and I'll totally show you around, what the actual fuck are you doing here?" I'm not angry, I'm in shock. I can only hope the smile on my face shows how happy I am to see him. I thought my best friend was a thing of the past, that we could never be close without the physical contact, but maybe I was wrong.

"Got a job in SoHo, we're completely converting one of the buildings into a restaurant. I thought I'd drop by to see your club, seeing as I'm only a ten-minute subway ride away."

"Ev didn't mention you were coming to do some work in The City when I spoke to him the other day. Bagel, please." I make grabby hands at him and he places the bag on the desk before sitting opposite me.

"Nah, it was a last-minute job. They called me and my guys in yesterday. Offered a lot of fucking money too. I'm not too proud to turn it down."

"Sold your soul to the big corporate man, did ya?"

With a bagel halfway to my mouth, I pause, realizing what he said about being in SoHo. It's where Marco's main New York hotel is. Gently shaking my head in disbelief at yet another coincidence in my fucked-up life, I let it go. Kai is working on a restaurant, not Marco's hotel.

"Want a tour then?" I stand, now–half-eaten bagel in hand, and round my desk. Kai moves from the chair and grabs me by the shoulders, pulling me in for one of his bear hugs, which settles something familiar in my soul. Even though they've never been as good as Everest's.

"Don't think you can get away without a hug, Psyche."

The scent of sandalwood fills my senses and I breathe in the comforting smell as I wrap my arms around him.

"Okay, that's enough. You're squishing my food. You know better than to mess with my food, Kai." We separate and he grabs a fresh bagel from the bag before joining me at the door.

"Ready to see my amazing club?" I'm excited about showing off this place to someone who really knows me. I'm proud as a motherfucker, and sharing things I love with people I love has always been something that has brought me joy.

The fact that this is the biggest thing I've ever done isn't something I'm taking lightly, and I suddenly feel giddy that I'm about to show Kai around this amazing achievement.

Sheryl and Lily practically drool over him as we head toward the entrance to the stairs that lead out to the main club, and it makes me smile how oblivious Kai is to it all. He has that Keanu Reeves vibe of just being naturally sexy without effort. A lot like Marco, actually, although he exudes a confidence unlike any other man I've ever known. Marco just needs to wink at me and it's like my pussy stands at attention. Fucking asshole.

Kai follows me down the stairs, eyes wide as he takes the place in. I try to imagine it from his point of view: the long bar on one side of the room and the huge stage dominating the space between the two staircases leading up to the mezzanine area; the mini stages dotted around the room with poles up to the ceiling; the luxurious seating areas, the dance floor, all decorated in red and black. It's a lot to take in and I can only imagine what a man like Kai is thinking about all this. He's never been a 'going out-out' kind of guy. Clubs, dancing, and parties have never been a Kai thing.

"Impressive, Riv. And all this is yours?" He's still looking around the room, gently nodding his head with a smile on his face.

"It is. Do you like it?"

"Fucking *like* it? It's amazing. I'm so proud of you, Riv." Grabbing my shoulder, he pulls me to him in a side hug as we survey my new kingdom.

I don't need his approval, but it's always a nice feeling when someone you care about has this kind of reaction to something you've worked hard for.

"Yeah, me too." I push him away playfully and he holds his arm as if I've just punched him, faking a moan of pain before we both laugh.

"Hey, Riv, I've got something I need to tell you." His face is suddenly serious again, those honey orbs holding me in place in anticipation.

"Okay..." I rest my ass against one of the round tables, my hands to either side of me as I wait for him to speak. Whatever it is isn't going to be easy for him to say, I can tell by the way he runs his fingers over his hair and rearranges his man bun.

"I wanna start by saying, I'm not trying to stir anything. This isn't me trying to do anything other than be your best friend."

"Spit it out, Kai." My voice is calm, and he knows me well enough to know that I think the build-up is almost worse than the actual thing.

"You know I'm working on that new restaurant. Well, it's practically opposite your husband's hotel." He takes a deep breath. "I saw a red-haired woman getting into an Aston Martin with your husband."

Jealousy isn't an emotion I'm familiar with, and I don't doubt Marco's intentions, but this bitch is getting on my last fucking nerve.

Elizabeth Ambrosio.

She's been a constant thorn in my side since she showed up a week ago. Apparently, her family has business dealings she's taking care of here in New York and Marco is the only one who can possibly help. After introducing herself to me as his fiancé, I refuse to make time for the woman. It was a total cunt move and she knew what she was doing. I don't have time for people like that. Though, I suppose it has given me something else to focus my mind on... other than, ya know, being a murderer.

If my heart was dark enough, I'd be all over sending Elizabeth to the bottom of the ocean, but that's not who I am and last time I checked, lust isn't a punishable offense. I still have enough light left inside me to know that would probably send me over the edge right alongside her.

Schooling my features to hide my semi-murderous thoughts, I give a tight smile. "Yeah, I know who that is.

Nothing to worry about, Kai. Though, I appreciate the heads up."

"Heads up to what?" That deep rumble is unmistakable, and I immediately push my thighs together for a little friction as Marco barges through the double doors at the main entrance, closely followed by a frowning Mimi, the head of my Rapture security team—she's almost like my own personal Enzo, only not as grumpy.

The artificial lighting in here only enhances the gloriousness that is Marco Mancini, his black shirt sleeves rolled up, showing off those porn-worthy forearms and the bulging biceps begging to be released. Dark hair styled in a perfect mess falling into his steel-gray eyes, which are currently piercing through me.

Kai's face drops even more, disappointment and defeat clear in his features. "I'm gonna go, Riv. But I'm working in the city for a couple months. Let's do a movie night sometime, yeah?"

"Abso-fucking-lutely. But you don't have to go."

"I've gotta get back to the crew anyway. See ya around, Psyche."

I stand as he leans in to hug me goodbye and I hear a growl from my left.

"Marco." Pulling away, Kai does that weird head-nod thing guys do as he says Marco's name.

"Kai." The head-nod is returned as Marco slides a possessive arm around my shoulders.

Turning, Kai heads toward the main entrance doors, where Mimi waves a hand in my direction to let me know she'll see him out.

Before he's even disappeared, Marco grasps the back of my head with one hand, my waist with the other, and slams his lips against mine. Without hesitation, I open up for him, the throbbing between my legs from his presence already making me aware of how wet I am.

I swear, I used to be the queen of restraint...

And this is just one reason that Marco is an asshole.

He keeps hold of my waist as he pulls away, looking down into my eyes and capturing my full attention with his serious expression.

*What is it with these men and being so sullen today?*

"What the fuck was Kai doing here, Tesoro?"

Oh no, he didn't!

"Don't give me that crap. I could ask the same to you." I raise an eyebrow in defiance at his gall.

"You think I'd know why Kai was here?" He mirrors my brow, a tilt appearing on one corner of his stupidly kissable mouth.

"You know what I mean, asshole. Did Elizabeth just fall into your car this morning?"

The lip-tilt has gone, and he furrows his brows, probably trying to figure out how I know.

He opens his mouth to speak before shaking his head in disbelief.

"Kai's working on the building across from my hotel." It's not a question, more a statement, like he has it all figured out.

"What's that got to do with anything?"

"He came over here to tell on me, didn't he?"

"No, actually. He brought me a bagel and wanted to look around."

"Yeah, and I saw several pigs flying through the sky an hour ago."

The smirk is back on his face, the playful glint in his eyes, and I find myself returning the expression.

"Whatever. That doesn't explain Elizabeth being in your car. I hope you made her sit in the back, or at least bleached the seat or something."

Marco full-on belly laughs and it's a fucking beautiful sound. He doesn't do it often enough, that control stick is up his ass a little too far sometimes.

"Your jealousy is sexy as fuck, Tesoro." He kisses my forehead gently. "Her driver was sick and she didn't give me a choice."

"Hmm."

"Now you know how I feel about that best friend of yours pawing all over you."

Before I can respond, his lips are on mine again, his palm cupping the back of my head in a possessive hold as his tongue battles for dominance with mine. It's a battle neither of us ever wins, but we both enjoy playing. My ass is still against the table and Marco nudges my legs apart to stand between them and get closer to me.

Gripping my ass, Marco lifts me to fully standing before unbuttoning the front of my pants. That's when I break our kiss to speak.

"Marco, what are you doing? We're in the middle of my club. Mimi is just outside the door."

"Don't give a fuck. Do you?" He continues kissing me, pressing his lips against my cheek, my chin, my neck, sending shivers of pure pleasure running up and down my spine.

I'm not afraid of public places, or getting caught, but I feel like I need to maintain some semblance of professionalism in my workplace.

But then again, the way his hands are stroking all over my body, and his lips are caressing my skin... the girls will understand.

Wrapping my arms around his neck, I let out a moan as Marco gently bites down on my shoulder.

"That's my good girl."

"Fuck off."

His breath tickles against my cheek as he chuckles and takes something from his suit jacket pocket before moving his hand down the front of my pants. When I feel the ball shapes sliding down the front of my pussy, I know what's coming... and it won't be me.

I know this man almost as well as I know myself, and that last *fuck off* I just gave him has sealed my fate.

The shock of two small balls entering me makes me gasp, just as Marco's mouth closes over mine, capturing my breathy inhale and responding with a growl.

He removes his hand, after spending a few seconds making sure my clit throbs for him, and holds my face in his palms.

"You can wear those until I take you to bed tonight, Tesoro. A reminder that you are mine, and I am yours. Fuck everyone else."

# Chapter Four

## Marco

"Which one is he?" Enzo's words hit their mark. With a side-eye in his direction, I let a smirk tick up on the side of my mouth as my gaze returns to the construction site across the street from my hotel.

My office is on the second floor, my view directly facing what I'm guessing is Kai Briggs's temporary workplace for the next few months. The owner of the building was a classmate of mine at Columbia, so calling him to chat and discreetly ask about his renovations was easy enough.

"None of those guys out there." I turn to look Enzo in the eye and grin. "Even so, I'm not stupid enough to tell you." River would have my balls if I let Enzo loose on her childhood friend.

"You're getting soft in your old married age."

With my hands in the pockets of my dress pants, I shrug at his words. Maybe I am when it concerns River, but I can't say I feel lesser for it. On the contrary, her presence in my life gives me strength in situations where in the past I would have just as easily sent Enzo in to deal with them. Having River by my side forces me to consider options that go against everything I was taught. Against everything a don should do. As the head of my family, I must protect us—always—but sometimes, violence can be avoided without it being a show of weakness.

"Not soft enough that I wouldn't throw you in the cellar and let you rot out the second half of your existence." Well, River isn't at my side right now, which means threats of violence are allowed.

The thought of my wife out there creating her own empire makes me smile with overflowing pride, but the feeling is brief as the main subject of our conversation walks out of the building, clipboard in hand and index finger pointing out into the distance.

"Christ, Boss, you just fucking growled like a savage. Guess I know who the guy is now."

There is nothing to say to that. He's right on all counts, but I refuse to be the instigator in this game Kai is trying to play. Little does he know or even understand that I don't lie to my wife. She's aware I'm keeping a secret, but even that will come to light soon. It has to. It's fucking time for her to know the whole story, she deserves the big picture.

This guy? Fuck, he let her go when they were teens. He chose his sex drive over his future, so as far as I'm concerned, he never deserved her. Hell, *I* don't fucking deserve her, but the only way I'm letting her go is if I'm lowered six feet under and covered in dirt.

"Walk with me." Turning on my heel, I swipe the documents from my desk and slide my favorite pen from the inside pocket of my suit jacket. "I need to make sure the hotel renovations are on schedule for the grand reopening."

Updating the SoHo location was a gamble, but my team has been working ridiculous overtime to make sure we don't lose too much money as our guests were transferred to our Upper West Side location. So far, miracles have happened and our timeline is being respected. Now, I just need to make sure my vision is coming to life.

"What's the situation with Elizabeth? Why is she back?" My questions are rapid fire because I need my second-in-command to keep me updated.

"I've had eyes on her, and for a while, there was nothing out of the ordinary. Until last night..." He pauses like this is a fucking soap opera and the producers just cut to commercial.

"And?"

"Gunner sent me pictures of her walking into Eleonor's gaudy mansion and not coming out until this morning, all fresh and ready for a new day." I come to a screeching halt and spin on my heel, the look on my face probably matching the anger in my tone.

"Why am I just hearing this now? You should have led with that instead of chit-chatting for the last hour." He snorts at my words, because Enzo doesn't chat. He drops bombs. In fact, he doesn't even acknowledge my outburst with a justification.

"Okay, so she's staying with Eleonor. That can't be a coincidence, which means she knows something or her family is planning something." My mind is whirring with the possibilities. As it stands, I'm the underboss of the most powerful family in New York City. I've got the resources, the contacts, loyal men working under me. They say it's lonely at the top, I say it's a constant position of danger. You're not lonely as much as you're vulnerable. So, when unfortunate coincidences show up—like Nathaniel's mother and the Ambrosio daughter playing house—it makes the hairs on my skin rise to full attention.

"Eleonor has been seen at the police station. She's asking around, demanding answers, but we covered all that. Normal reaction, I'd say. Anything less would be a red flag. As far as any and all digital footprints are concerned, Nate decided to take a last-minute trip to offer his medical services to those in need in Nigeria." Slowing his gait, Enzo takes out his phone and in a flurry of flying thumbs, sends off a text then puts his phone back in his pocket.

"What are our eyes and ears in Naples saying?"

"There's rumbling, some rumors about you and Elizabeth joining forces." Fuck. These assholes won't give up, will they?

"Put an end to it. The only way my union to River is dissolved is if one of us is dead."

"Done." Just as he says the word, my phone rings. The screen flashes the name of my father and I know I can't ignore it. My mother calls to catch up, my father calls for business.

"*Buon giorno, Papà, come stai?*" My father and I are close. We share the hot-blooded heritage that sometimes boils just under the surface, which means our conversations often get loud and gesticulative. Despite the world in which I've had to grow up, my life has been one of privilege and love.

"*Figlio mio, sto bene, grazie.*" Every time I ask him how he's doing he always—always—answers the same. That he's fine. Even when a hit was put on his head, he had told me, "My son, I'm fine, thank you." The truth could only be found in his tone.

"We need to talk about this Elizabeth mess."

I'm careful not to sigh at my father's words as I take the stairs down to the ground floor with Enzo right behind me. It's clear my father means business since the conversation continues in his native tongue.

"I'm handling it." I snap my fingers to get our architect's attention then point to a crack in the banister. I don't want anyone overlooking a single detail of these renovations. There's no excuse for a luxury hotel to be less than pristine. My clients won't stand for it, and neither will I.

"Not enough. She called your mother, and you know I don't like to see your mother upset." By 'upset' he means pissed off, which is exactly what I'm feeling right now.

Looking over at Enzo as we walk through the door and into the grand hall, I mouth, "Get me Elizabeth on the phone, now."

"I'll take care of it," I repeat, trying to stay cryptic like my father taught me. 'Never speak freely on the phone, son.'

"Her family is upset about your last conversation with Eric at the Christmas Eve party." His voice is tight, like he's reeling in his irritation at the whole situation—one my parents instigated by promising the Ambrosios that our families would be united. Now, I have to clean up the fucking mess I created when I fell in love with River and didn't give a fuck who knew or what consequences I had to face. It's why a long engagement wasn't an option. The Ambrosios were planning a lavish wedding and once I found River, it was imperative I put a stop to it all. With the added benefit of having the woman I've pined over, irrefutably mine.

She's worth it.

She's worth everything.

"Maybe they shouldn't have raised such an asshole." The Italian word for asshole is *stronzo*, and it's a great, strong-sounding word with hard consonants and masculine intent.

"Watch your language. Your mother has you on speaker phone." I try not to laugh but a chuckle escapes anyway. My mother refuses to not be in the loop and a conversation with her children without her hearing it is unacceptable.

"*Ciao, Mamma.*"

"*Ciao, bellissimo.*"

For the next five minutes, I listen and respond to my mother's excitement about this thing or another, reassuring her that River and I are, indeed, joining them in the

Hamptons for Easter. That is, until my entire focus hones in on the tall, broad figure that's walking up to the hotel entrance.

*Motherfucker.*

"Son, just remember, whatever you choose to do, we stand with you. Keep your head on your shoulders and don't be too quick with your temper." I'm listening to my father's words and registering the urgency of his meaning, but I find it funny how he's talking about my temper just as Kai Briggs struts into my fucking hotel like he owns it.

"*Baci*, Mamma. I have to go." I don't hang up until they both say their goodbyes, but my mind is already finding the hundred and one different ways that can I make this fucker scream without actually killing him.

Not that I don't want to, but it would upset River, and that's unacceptable.

"I believe you've walked into the wrong renovation job." Sliding my hands into the pockets of my slacks, I play the role of nonchalance. I keep my emotions in check and study his body language, the tone of his voice, the intent behind his words.

"Nice place. A bit too lavish for us though." He's dressed exactly as one would expect him to be while working construction. Dirty from head to toe, with shit kickers he didn't bother to stomp at the entrance. Little prick.

"By 'us' you mean your work crew?" I know exactly who he means but, again, I'm trying to be a gentleman by not ripping his head right off.

"My family. Everest, Petal, *River*." I notice he leaves out his wife's name and I'm not sure if it's because he doesn't quite consider her family or because she would absolutely love staying in a place like this.

With a chuckle, I lower my head and raise my eyes at him, my smirk fully in place at the bullshit he just spewed.

"Right, right. So, what can I do for you, Kai? Looking to spend a couple of nights with your wife? I'm sure I could get you a good price on the honeymoon suite." I shrug like it's no big deal. "I know the owner."

"Cut the shit, Marco. I saw you the other day with that redhead and I may have fucked up with River,"—I feel Enzo walk up behind me by the violent energy he gives off when any type of threat is close—"but I'll be damned if I let you hurt her."

Raising my hand to stop Enzo from doing anything rash, I cock my head to the side and take a step closer to the man standing in front of me. Where he has me in width, I tower in height, but to his credit, he doesn't back down, which tells me he's serious about wanting to protect my wife.

Too little, too late though, isn't it?

"I can assure you, River is not and will never be hurt by me in that way." He scoffs at my words until I shut it all down. "Why would I ever look elsewhere when I have perfection at the tip of my fingers?"

His posturing falters just enough for me to see it. Because, yeah, he let her go. He fucked up and will regret that move for the rest of his life.

"I'm watching you."

"I'll be sure to offer you some binoculars for your next birthday."

Kai's lip actually curls at my sarcasm. "I'm warning you, Mancini, I will protect her at all costs."

*Hmm, where was that promise when she really needed you?*

"That, right there, Kai Briggs, shows me you don't know her." Kai steps closer, his jaw clenching, but knowing damn well this isn't a fair fight. "River doesn't need your protection. She needs your support. She's a queen not a princess."

He points his index finger at me for good measure, provoking a growl from Enzo before taking a step back and walking away.

Young pups. They don't understand the subtlety of a good threat.

"I'd end him, but I don't need River pissed off at me." My head snaps to the right, my gaze searching Enzo's features.

"Since when do you care what River thinks? I thought you didn't like her?" I can count on the fingers of one hand the number of people Enzo truly trusts.

"I like her just fine."

I grin at him, because that's practically a declaration of brotherly love coming from him.

"Good to know."

# Chapter Five
## River

Other than spending last Sunday with Ev and Petal, I've kept my mind focused on work and Marco since what happened in my apartment. I know I'll never be the same again, but I also know I'm learning to live with what I've done. And for once, I'm not trying to do it alone.

Marco Mancini has opened up a whole new world to me, and while it's scary sometimes, I'm never actually afraid when I'm with him. I've found a new side to myself that I never imagined I needed.

Yes, I'm a murderer twice over now, which is fucked up beyond all belief, and I probably have something very wrong with me to not be in pieces over it all, but that's never been a *me* thing. I'm not completely unfeeling though. I allow myself a few moments every day to feel the shame before picking myself up again and moving on, reminding myself that I didn't choose these outcomes.

I am a *survivor* of these outcomes.

Marco has this way of encouraging me to thrive. He is a controlling asshole most of the time, but even then, I hold all the cards. It's a heady feeling, knowing that this powerful man would go to his knees for me if only I ask. And I don't take that lightly. Not anymore.

I know I've been trying to deny my own feelings—very unsuccessfully—but with every passing day, my walls are breaking down, and I'm realizing that doing it all on my own isn't what I want anymore. Polly was right when she told me about finding the other half of your soul. *You'll never be the same again once you've found them.*

The rumble of the Aston's engine as we pull off from a stop sign brings me back to the here and now and I smile as Marco gently squeezes my hand on his thigh before bringing it to his lips and kissing my knuckles.

He doesn't speak or take his eyes from the road, but the simple gesture is everything to me in this moment. It's as if he has a sixth sense capable of tapping into my thoughts.

This time last year, the idea of being this way—for real—with anyone was akin to finding a giant golden unicorn in the street. But now... that giant golden unicorn is driving me in his red Aston Martin to stay with his parents in the Hamptons for Easter weekend.

I haven't told him with my words how I feel yet. For one, fucking with him is one of my new favorite hobbies, and second, it hasn't felt like the right time. It's a big-ass deal for me to say those three little words to anyone who isn't my family, and it's only these last couple of weeks I've admitted it to myself. I know he's still keeping some secrets from me, but I'm hoping that he comes clean sooner rather than later.

In fact, I plan on confronting him once this weekend with his parents is over. Get everything out in the open, once and for all. Complete honesty from both of us about everything. Well, not everything. The secrets I have with Lina are hers to tell.

"We're here, Tesoro."

Marco cuts the engine and gets out of the car while I take a deep breath, because meeting his parents at a party in passing was fine, even spending some time with them on our wedding day was fine, but spending the whole weekend with them? Yeah, a girl needs a breath. The passenger door is open before I can exhale and Marco leans in to unbuckle my seatbelt, taking the opportunity to smell and nip at my neck.

"Hey!" I slap him away and he chuckles lowly as he stands, reaching out his hand to help me out of the car.

Not that I need it, but I'm guessing he's playing the part of the perfect gentleman, seeing as the front door of the beautiful house is now open and his mom is heading in our direction.

She envelops him in her arms before pulling back to kiss each of his cheeks as she greets him. Then she sets her sights on me. A comforting feeling of home sets in with her arms around me, and suddenly some of my anxieties about being here fall away. It's quite the welcome, but Mrs. Mancini has always been really friendly toward me.

"It's been so long since my boy's come to stay with us for a holiday. I always knew he just needed a woman's hand. *Grazie*, River." She winks at me as she pulls away and begins walking back toward the house. "I've had the guest house prepared for you, but first, you're coming inside with me. Your Papà is on the back porch with the dog."

Marco chuckles beside me, reaching out to take my hand in his. "You ready for this, Tesoro?" He's smirking and I know this is a rhetorical question. Whether I'm ready or not, this is happening. Three days and two nights. At least we'll be in the guest house and not technically under the same roof as Marco's parents. Silver lining and all that.

"As I'll ever be." Rolling my eyes, I smirk right back at him.

The afternoon sunlight shines through the blanket of trees surrounding us, giving Marco's golden skin a stunning glow and lighting up the smile on his annoyingly perfect face.

A tiny dark-brown Pomeranian pitter-patters across to us when we enter the living room attached to the back porch by large sliding glass doors.

"Hey, little guy." No hesitation, I let go of Marco's hand and bend down to fuss over the little fluffy dog who is currently sniffing my ankle.

"His name is Bruce." Marco speaks from behind me. I can hear the smile in his voice, but I don't look up, too busy with this little cutie. He jumps up at me, his tiny paws on my bare leg as he wags his tail, and now I'm a little sad that I'm wearing a dress today because I can't move around on the floor too much without giving an ass show.

Reluctantly standing, I'm met with Marco at my back as he slides a hand around my waist to my stomach, resting it there as he whispers into my neck.

"Don't pout, Tesoro. I'll give you something to stroke when I get you alone." With a nip at my earlobe, he encourages me to move forward, out onto the porch where his parents are waiting for us.

I want to roll my eyes again, but it'd be useless because he can't see me... and what good is rolling my eyes at him if I'm not going to get punished for it later?

The traditional Italian Easter is not too dissimilar to something my own family would do. We spent Friday evening by candlelight after a moment's silence at five pm, which is apparently the time of the Pope's Holy Friday mass. Lina had shown up with thirty minutes to spare, Enzo trailing behind her, and between us, we all got through far too many bottles of wine. It may not be my favorite drink, but when around Italians, you drink wine.

Yesterday was a fun day. Marco and I spent most of it by the lake with Lina and Enzo, drinking more wine and eating too much food. His parents had watched with loving eyes from the back porch, reminding me of how my parents used to watch Ev and I when we would run around for hours on end, climbing trees and causing our own kind of mischief.

For what is technically considered a crime family, mafia and all that, they're surprisingly down to Earth. I don't know what I was expecting before we came here, to be honest, but I'm having a really good time with them. It's so peaceful here, with the huge lake in their backyard and the trees surrounding the house and grounds, it's secluded from the rest of the world, and while I'm here, I don't miss The City at all.

I may also have a new-found appreciation for boats after receiving more orgasms than I can count in the Mancinis' 'small' speed boat as we bobbed along the water.

Today, I'm in the kitchen with Lina and Gabriella, Marco's mom, dying eggs in beet water, getting them ready to go with our lamb dinner this afternoon. Bruce is like a little shadow, getting under our feet as we move around, but he's too cute to get frustrated with.

"Bruce, *sdraiato.*" Gabriella waves her wooden spoon around, and she's said this enough times over the weekend for me to know she's just told the dog to go and lie down.

I chuckle as he dutifully turns away from her legs and heads toward the corner of the kitchen. I'm sure he has a dog bed in every room of this place.

"Okay, I think we're all done, ladies."

"Finally! Can we eat now, Mamma? I'm starving." Lina is hungover as fuck and even several cups of coffee this morning hasn't helped. She's clearly still feeling rough.

Gabriella asked us both to help her prepare what we could before breakfast, another family tradition she insisted I join in with.

"*Si.*" She smiles at her daughter affectionately, with a small shake of her head. "Get the *pastiera* from the pantry and we'll go join the men at the breakfast table."

Lina dutifully does as she's been asked as I wash my hands. "Do you need me to take anything through, Gabriella?"

"No, that's the last of it. You are a good girl, aren't you." It's not a question, it's a statement, and she side-hugs me as she begins walking out of the kitchen, mumbling under her breath. "Just like her…"

It immediately reminds me of her comment at the Christmas party and, call me curious, but I need to know what she's talking about.

"Wait, Gabriella…"

She pauses in the doorway and looks over her shoulder. "*Si?*"

"What do you mean by, *just like her*?"

I may as well have just shot Bruce with the way she balks. Her eyes widen, and she can't seem to find the words she needs. She's close to tears, and I go to move toward her for a hug—I didn't mean to upset her—but before I can move, she surprises me with a trick I know all too well: masking.

Her features soften, her eyebrows drop, and she simply says, "Oh, it's nothing." Then she turns and leaves the kitchen, leaving me dumbfounded as to why this sweet older lady would straight-up lie to me like that.

Although... mafia wife. I should expect nothing less than the unexpected in this world.

It's frustrating as Hell, because I really want to know, and now my thoughts are spiraling...

Maybe it has something to do with what Marco is keeping from me? I fucking hope so anyway. All these pieces of random information are being dropped at my feet and I'm trying desperately to put them all together, but then I have to question if it's even worth it.

Things are going okay right now...

Ah, for fuck's sake. I'm not and never have been a head-in-the-sand girl. I need to know all the things.

As soon as we are in the car on the way home tomorrow, I'm speaking to Marco. He can't distract me with orgasms or anything while he's driving. He'll have no choice but to talk.

Bruce follows me out of the kitchen as I head to the sun-room for their traditional Easter Sunday breakfast. Apparently, the Pastiera Napoletana represents the birth of the savior. While I may not be Catholic and have the same beliefs, I can appreciate the ritual of it all, and the way something like Easter brings the family together can only be a beautiful thing.

Paws scratching quickly along the floor catches my attention—Bruce is an older dog, so moving this quickly isn't something I've seen him do in my time here. I watch him scramble through the hall to join us before he begins howling.

Maybe he's excited for breakfast?

The sight before me as I enter the room makes me freeze. It all seems to happen at once. There's an almighty crash and Marco's face is turning white, full of panic as he watches his dad, who is clutching at his left arm, fall from his chair. He moves so fast, barely catching Alberto before he hits the floor. Gabriella drops the glass she's holding and holds her hands up to her face. Lina throws the serving spoon she was using behind her as she stands and rushes to move to her dad. Enzo is somehow already by Alberto and Marco, helping to gently lie the old man down.

"Daddy!"

"Alberto!"

"Enzo, call an ambulance."

Everyone speaks at the same time, the dog is barking, and all I feel is guilt.

Guilt because I was finally going to get some answers, and it seems the universe has other ideas. Every time I get anywhere close to information that's being kept from me, something shitty happens to push it out of everyone's mind.

I'd say needing an ambulance for your dad on Easter Sunday takes priority over giving me answers, and I feel like a selfish bitch for even thinking of myself while this is all going on.

With a deep breath, I take in the situation and ready myself for another rough few days. These people are mine now, and they're hurting. So I'm going to do what I do best, which is take care of my family.

# Chapter Six
## Marco

I read somewhere that, in the U.S., the average death rate in a hospital is about thirty-five percent. So, as we sit in the waiting room while the nurses and doctors on the other side of the 'No Entry' door try to save my father's life, I think about those statistics. I think about the fact that sixty-five percent of people who come in, get to walk out.

My father is only sixty years old. He can beat this. He's survived vendettas against him, this is nothing compared to the will of an Italian with a grudge.

"Do you want some coffee? Or something to eat? What can I do for you?" I slide my gaze to the right. My gorgeous wife is worried, doting on me like the thought of me being in pain physically hurts *her*.

Palming the side of her face, my heart constricts as she presses into my hand and closes her eyes. It's such a tender moment, and although I'm trying to reassure her that everything is going to be okay, I'm the one who's recharged. Her tenderness is my morphine. I crave it, every morsel she gives.

"All I need is you, Tesoro. Right here next to me." My words are whispered so I don't disturb the others waiting on their loved ones. After all, thirty five percent of us here will have bad news. It makes sense why hospitals are always dreaded, but I have to focus on the fact that a hundred years ago, those odds were reversed.

So, here's to modern medicine and the fact that it's going to save my dad.

"Mrs. Mancini?" We all rise as one when my mother is called by the doctor who's just pulled his scrub cap off. He looks tired, like saving my father's life took a toll on his own well-being. If only he knew how many men my father put *in* the hospital, I wonder if he would have worked as hard to save him...

"Yes, Doctor. These are my children, you can speak freely." Nodding at us all, he directs his next words at my mother alone.

"Your husband suffered a major heart attack. We were able to go in and repair the damage to the left anterior artery and also remove the blood clot that essentially provoked the attack." My mother—whose hand is gripping my wrist, her nails doing some serious damage—relaxes the tiniest fraction at his words. I'm hoping he's not throwing all these terms at us just to announce my father is dead.

"Okay, so that means?" It's my turn to hold my mother because the doctor's next words will either allow her to breathe or break her completely.

"He's in the ICU, the next twenty-four hours are critical, but we're hopeful that he'll make a full recovery *if...*"—his dramatic pause makes me want to shake the theatrics out of him—"he follows treatment and changes his eating habits."

*Yeah, good luck with that.*

My mother's entire body melts at the good news, like now she can breathe and smile and live again. "Thank you, Doctor. Can we see him?"

"In a little while. Right now he needs the rest, but I'll send a nurse out to get you when he's wheeled into his own room."

I shake the hand of the man who's just saved my father's life before I turn to my mother and envelop her in my embrace. She's not crying, never in public places, but I know that once she's in the room with him or at home, she'll break down. It's her process and I've learned to deal with it.

"No more fats and *salsiccia* for Papà, huh?" She chuckles at that then lifts her delicate features to meet my gaze, her inner strength clear in the spark of her gray eyes. Eyes so much like mine.

"*Vedremo, figlio mio, vedremo.*"

And I suppose we *will* see, but we will also act. I'm not going through this emotional wringer again and I'm definitely not watching my mother suffer the way she has the past several hours since he fell at their dining room table.

Patting my cheek with tenderness only a mother can gift, her attention is stolen by the other most important woman in my life.

"Gabriella." In that one word, River says everything.

*I'm sorry you had to go through that.*

*I'm happy it all worked out.*

*Let me give you a hug.*

I hear it all in those four syllables.

They hug and my mother squeezing my wife like her own daughter provokes a strange feeling of pride right where my heart beats. But it's when her eyes meet mine over River's shoulder that I hear everything she's not saying.

My mother loves my wife.

I push my hands into the front pockets of my jeans and raise a brow at the woman who raised me, a silent answer in my eyes.

"*Anche io, Mamma.*" Me too, Mamma, me fucking too.

Lina is burrowed in Enzo's embrace, watching the scene, when she, too, looks up at me. Except, instead of telling me she loves River, she's threatening me.

"Don't fuck this up." Her silent words are mouthed behind my mother's back. I wink at her, knowing damn well that I probably will fuck up. My only saving grace is that I will always make it up to her.

"Well, I'm going to make sure the paperwork is settled so your father can have a private room. We don't want innocent people having to deal with his attitude." My father is a proud man and being told to lie down and rest is akin to telling him he's weak and useless.

"Okay, I'm going to get some fresh air with River. We'll be right back." River's fingers all too naturally weave into mine as I lead her downstairs and outside into the crisp spring night air.

"Are you all right?"

Am I? I'm not sure. But then I pull my wife into my chest and inhale the sweet scent of her lavender essential oils and decide that yes, I am okay. It was a close call, but we can fix this. As long as I have River by my side, we can fix anything.

"Oh, I know what you need." River takes my hand and pulls me to the park across the street. It's nearly two in the morning, not a soul in sight, with the only lighting coming from the streetlights.

"A blowjob?" I'm only half kidding. No one would see us out here. We could probably even get a little quickie to relax us both.

"No, you fiend."

*Well, that's disappointing.*

I sigh theatrically, like she's just ruined my entire year, which earns me a grunt and a slap across my chest.

"Behave." I chuckle at her word choice. It seems I'm rubbing off on her.

"That's my line." I stop in my tracks and pull her into me, steadying her when she almost loses her footing.

"I love you, River Fox-Mancini." My hands frame her gorgeous face as I peer into the depths of her green orbs. Chances are, she's going to destroy me with her next words, but that's okay. The greatest part of loving someone is offering your vulnerability without expecting anything in return.

"You know, someday I'm going to believe you." I grin at her admission. She didn't destroy me, she gave me hope.

"That day can't come soon enough." I kiss her then. It's tender and it's real. It's all the words and all the promises.

"Come on, Romeo." I groan as she leads me to wherever, or whatever, she thinks will make me feel better. Apparently, inside her hot, tight cunt isn't the right answer.

After walking for what feels like three lifetimes, we are in the exact middle of no-fucking-where, which is the exact place River chooses to stop, turning to me with a huge grin on her face.

"Now, don't panic." Fucking Hell, this will not end well.

"You realize those words have the opposite effect, right?" I'm looking around, wondering if I should have brought my gun with me.

"Yes, but still. This is going to feel so good. I promise." I groan again because cock in pussy still isn't on the menu, apparently.

"The only thing that'll feel good is—" She places her index finger on my lips and frowns.

"Do not finish that sentence, Marco. I'm trying to be good here."

"Let me reassure you,"—I kiss the pad of her finger then suck it into my mouth before biting the end—"you are at your best when I'm fucking the sass right out of you." River's only answer is a growl, bared teeth and all, before she turns, offering me her perfect profile, and does the last thing I expect her to do.

She screams.

Like, full on someone-is-trying-to-murder-me-in-a-Halloween-movie scream. Immediately, I scan the entire area to make sure cops aren't going to descend on me and throw me in jail.

"What the fuck, River?" I whisper-yell, my hand flying to her mouth to quiet her down. It's as I'm doing it that I realize my action could be misconstrued if anyone *did* show up to save my Little Miss Trouble.

Pulling my hand down, she turns to me and grins.

"I swear, it feels so good. All the stress just flies away." In this very moment, under the high beams of the crescented moonlight, River looks so young. So hopeful. She looks like the carefree girl she should have grown up to be.

My heart constricts knowing my world very nearly destroyed her world. I may not have killed her parents, but someone did. Someone who wanted her dead too.

Someone who is still gunning for her.

"Try it. I promise, it'll help." Her hands rest on my chest, her fingers curling around my shirt and pulling me to her so she can whisper dirty words to me. "I'll deepthroat you right here and now if you do it."

I grin, shaking my head at her because she knows exactly how to get her way.

Little Miss Trouble, indeed.

"Fine."

She squeals. Fucking *squeals,* like I've given her the best birthday gift imaginable.

Facing the same stand of trees she did, I take in a deep breath and, before I can think better of it, let out a cry that makes the small animals scatter.

In that moment, I empty myself of my frustration. My worries. My responsibilities.

I exorcise my sins and my lies, the truths I'm withholding vanish into the darkness, and my head clears for a brief second in time.

Just as my lungs burn with the lack of oxygen, I lean forward—my hands on my knees—and heave in breath after breath.

"So?" Shaking my head at my eager little wife, I turn to face her before rising to my full height. My lungs burn like they've run a marathon and my heart feels like it's about to burst wide open.

"Is this the part where I admit defeat?" I have her in my arms again, my hand splayed across the small of her back, when she closes the already tiny space that separates us.

"No, silly. This is the part where you trust that I'll always have your back." Staring at her, utterly lost in her depths, especially with the dim lighting out here, I try my best to keep this moment sacred.

"Is that right?"

"Yes, Mr. Mancini. You don't have to be some kind of titan. I'm a badass bitch with large shoulders and great ideas." Pushing her chin up with my thumb, I tilt my head enough to lick a path through her parted lips and delve deep into her mouth for a mind-blowing kiss.

Her arms circle my neck, her entire body molded to mine as my cock recognizes that I might just get my wish tonight—outdoors and by the light of the moon. It feels symbolic or something, like her witchy ways have seeped into my soul.

River moans and I swallow her sounds, take them deep inside myself, when my phone rings and utterly destroys all my filthy plans with my wife. I can't ignore it, not with my entire family at the hospital and my father recuperating from a massive heart attack.

"You should get that." My wife, always thinking of others.

"Lina, is everything okay?" I lick my lips, savoring the taste of my queen as I rub my thumb across her mouth.

"Yeah, they said we can go in and see him. He should be waking up any time now."

"Okay, we'll be right there. Thank you." I end the call, a little disappointed that our bubble has dissipated but equal parts eager to see my father.

"Let's go, big guy. Papà Mancini needs our support."

Christ, I love this woman.

"*Basta*, Gabri. I'm fine, stop fussing." My father traps my mother's hand in his as she tries to cover him up with the hospital blanket just as I walk in the room with River at my side.

"Papà, let her dote on you or else she'll take it out on me." I lean over him, squeezing his free hand, and whisper in his ear. "Don't do that again. Too close of a call."

Shrugging, he chuckles like it was nothing.

"I've survived worse. I'm not dying of a damn heart attack." Turning to my mother, he holds her with his don stare. Little does he know, that look hasn't scared my mother in ages, if ever. "I won't give up my *salsiccia*." I roll my eyes as my mother nods. That's code for, "We'll see," which means she'll get her way.

When a nurse walks in, my mother gives her the necessary space to do whatever it is she needs to do, standing beside me and River.

"I'm going to step out, get us some coffee." I kiss River on the forehead as a thank you and reluctantly let go of her hand. "Glad you're better, Papà Mancini." The room snorts and my father's face erupts in a great big smile. Oh, he likes that one.

"I want my grandbabies to call me that," he booms out to River, who just pretends she didn't hear him. "*Mi hai sentito?*"

"She hears you, Papà, and is choosing to ignore you. Plus, she doesn't understand Italian."

"You need to teach her, Son. Your children must learn our family language." Yeah, yeah, this conversation is not fit for a hospital room.

Enzo walks in with Lina and as soon as I see him, I feel the ice of his presence. He loves my father like his own and seeing him like this hurts him as much as it hurts me.

"What are you doing?" Following his gaze, I see the nurse checking my father's IV bags, taking notes on her tablet and fussing over the needles. She's so busy with her job she doesn't even realize Enzo's speaking to her. "Hey!" At that, she looks up, startled, then looks around the room.

"Me? I'm making sure he's got his morphine and fluids." She's flustered and I feel bad for her. Enzo can be a lot, but it always comes from a good place. Of course, he doesn't apologize, just grunts like a fucking caveman.

"Sorry, we're a little on edge." River is teaching me to apologize. That was my attempt and I think she'd be proud.

"No problem. I'll just leave you to it." Taking all of her equipment, she bows her head and scuttles out the door.

"Christ, Enzo, nurses are the lifeline of a hospital. Do not ever piss them off," Lina scolds him in a whisper-yell before she walks over to my father and kisses him on the cheek. "You look good, Papà." She's lying and everyone knows it. He's pale and tired but he's alive and I'm okay with that.

"I need to speak to Marco before these meds make me sleep again."

Enzo nods, leaving with Lina after she kisses our father again. Mother fusses just a little more until my dad kisses her knuckles—all four—then lingers on her wedding band.

"*Ti amo, Cucciola.*" I never understood his term of endearment for my mother—calling her a cub seemed strange—until I found River and realized certain words should hold meaning only for them.

"*Ti amo tanto, amore mio.*" They hold each other's gazes as she pats his hand then smiles up at me. I feel like an intruder, but I was raised in this environment, where loving your spouse is more important than anything else in the world.

Once we're alone, my father's bravado suddenly evaporates. He's exhausted.

"We can have this conversation later. You need to get some rest." He tuts at me, waving off my concerns like they're based off of nothing.

"Have you told her?"

Fuck. This now?

"No."

"Okay, you need to tell her. Everything, Marco. Life is too short. Also, the Napolitanos aren't going to sit back and take it. You have to be proactive. Always watch your back. I'll support you in whatever way I can. Got it?"

I nod, knowing damn well that he's too beat for this kind of conversation. "*Si, capisco.*"

"*Bene, bene.* Now, let me sl—" As his eyes roll to the back of his head, all fucking Hell breaks loose in the room.

It starts with the beeping of the machine, followed by an ominous voice repeating "Code Blue" over and over again. From that moment on, people start running into his room, pushing me aside as they move around like they've done this a million times. I'm asked to wait outside and I'm too shocked to even argue, walking backwards with my eyes fixed on my father's limp body.

What the fuck is happening? He was just cracking jokes and telling my mother he loved her. One doctor is doing CPR, her entire body pressing on his chest over and over again, while another is heating up the paddles.

"Two hundred."

"Two hundred."

"Clear."

Suddenly, everyone's hands are in the air as the doctor places the paddles right where his chest was open wide mere hours ago.

"No pulse."

"Give me three hundred."

"Three hundred."

"Clear."

Again with the raised hands, but nothing has changed. His body is still limp, his eyes closed. His skin a pasty color that does not belong to our family.

"Again."

"Three hundred."

"Clear."

The sound of the shock isn't nearly as deafening as the sound of Lina's gasp. I don't dare look behind me. I can't face my mother, my sister. Enzo. Fuck, where's River?

"Asystole."

No. This can't be right. The long, uninterrupted beep that accompanies the word throws me.

Did I say Lina's gasp was deafening? Fuck, how I was wrong.

The sound of my father flatlining is a memory I'll never get over.

"Time of death,"—the doctor looks at her watch, then at my father's body—"five fifty-three a.m."

Worse than the flatline is my mother's wail, her deep, wrenching pain that paralyzes everyone in a fifty-foot radius.

Enzo holds Lina as her knees give out and I rush to my mother as she lets herself fall to the ground.

"Marco?" I lift my head to see my beautiful wife carrying three coffees, confusion etched across her features.

The doctors stand before us, tired and resigned. "We're sorry for your loss."

"No. Nooooo. He was fine. *Amore mio*, wake up. He was fine. Marco, please, he's just sleeping." I hold my mother as close as I can to my chest, watching as River places the cups on the nearest table and rushes over to the other side of me. We don't say anything, there are absolutely no words that could possibly soothe my mother right now. Not a single one. I know, because I can't imagine anything soothing the deep ache inside my chest.

Except River.

She looks up at me like she knows I'm seeking out her healing touch. Her free hand goes to my cheek, my eyes close for the briefest of moments and I feel her power seep into me, giving me enough strength to take care of my family.

Somewhere in the commotion, I hear Enzo demand the names of everyone who was in the room and everything that was administered to my dad. It's our protocol, our way to make sure this wasn't a hit.

Except we all know who the culprit is.

Stress and a rich diet.

The widow-maker's perfect storm.

# CHAPTER SEVEN

## RIVER

"I think I can feel the baby moving around every now and then. There are these flutters, and one of the baby books Ev brought home from the library says it could be movements or gas. I'm choosing to believe the former, of course. Oh, Riv, pregnancy is just the most wonderful thing." Petal sighs down the line and I can just picture her whimsical little doll-face as she describes what's going on inside her body. But also...

"Wait a minute, Pet. You're telling me that my brother actually went into a library?"

Bruce nuzzles his nose into my thigh where I'm sitting on the soft, deep-blue sofa in the main living room. He, along with Gabriella, came to stay at Marco's after the funeral a couple weeks ago. I fuss his furry little head as he begs for attention.

Petal's fairy-like giggle practically twinkles through the phone. "I know, I had to check his temperature when he told me where he'd been, just to make sure he wasn't ill."

"I bet the librarian had a shock when he walked in."

"He made Kai go with him. Poor woman probably thought all her wildest book boyfriend dreams had come true when they approached the counter." Her laugh is infectious and I can do nothing but join her. Bruce's little black eyes watch me with some kind of cute doggy fascination before he jumps onto my legs and settles in my lap.

"Oh, to be a fly on the wall. That's some funny shit. How's the hunt for a doula coming along?"

"We've narrowed it down to three, so we're going to spend some time with each of them over the next few weeks to see which one fits with us." While she's speaking, I hear Ev's whispering voice in the background. "Hang on a second, Riv." There are some rustling noises, followed by Petal's giggle and some more rustling, and I continue to stroke Bruce's soft fur while I wait. "Sorry, Riv. Gotta go, Bear just came home for a lunch break an—"

"Pet, please don't finish that sentence." I laugh, because I do not want to hear about what my brother wants to *eat* on his lunch break. No thank you.

"Good point. I love you, Gorgeous, but yeah... See you in a couple days?"

"Absolutely. I'm looking forward to seeing how my niece or nephew is growing in that beautiful belly of yours. Love you both."

"Love you too. Byeee."

Ending the call, I put my cell on the arm of the sofa and lean my head back, closing my eyes. It's been a tough few weeks, and since we have Marco's mom living here, he's barely had any time to just relax. He's constantly in dutiful-son mode, which is a beautiful thing, and I do what I can to help, but I can tell he's struggling. So in the spirit of giving this whole being an actual loving wife thing a go, I insisted he come with me this weekend. Although, he didn't take much persuading.

A bonfire with blankets, hot chocolate, and marshmallows may not be his first idea of a relaxing night, but there's just something that an evening in the outdoors like that does to a person's insides. It was Petal's idea, which made me smile when she told me. This means she likes him, even after everything.

"River?" Bruce's little ears perk up at the sound of Lina's voice coming from the hall.

"In here."

"That's the trouble with so many rooms, it takes forever to find anyone. Enzo's waiting outside in the car. You ready?" Lina appears in the doorway of the TV room looking impeccable—as always—in a fitted black skirt ending mid-calf, a black crop-top, and three-inch stiletto sandals. Her long, dark hair is effortlessly styled, swept off to one side in loose waves, and her signature red lipstick completes her sophisticated look.

It's nice to see her wearing it again after so many weeks. I get it, losing a parent is fucking hard, and she may be having a good day today, but that doesn't mean she's suddenly okay. We've spoken several times since it happened, had our fair share of deep conversations, and as someone who has lost her parents, I know it never gets easier, you just learn how to live with it. And that takes time, like everything else that's difficult or shitty.

"I am ready. Just gotta put my shoes on and I'm all yours." Picking Bruce up off my lap, I nuzzle into his cute little face as I stand before passing him on to Lina. "Can we bring him with us?"

"Not where we're going, it's too fancy."

"Ooh, nice. Give me two secs and I'll see you by the front door."

Giving her a peck on each cheek, and a fur ruffle for Bruce, I run upstairs to grab my shoes. I've been wearing less name-brand clothes lately. With nobody to impress while I'm working, my own simple business-chic style has become my new favorite.

"I have a gift for you, Tesoro."

Marco's deep growl sends tingles down my spine every time. *I wonder if I'll ever tire of the feeling?*

Still buckling my shoe, I turn to face him in the doorway to our room. He has one hand holding the top of the jamb, while the other is in his pants pocket; his black shirt sleeves are rolled up, showcasing the beautiful cross tattoo that has a special place in my spank-bank on his porn-worthy forearm; and his smile... well, it melts my panties every freaking time when paired with his lust-filled eyes. The dark circles underneath them are a testament to how little he's been sleeping, but there is no cure for grief.

"As much as I love a gift, Enzo is in the car waiting to take me and Lina to our lunch date."

"Oh, I know." He raises that goddamn sexy eyebrow at me as he pulls his hand out of his pocket, presenting me with my gift...

"Absolutely not, Mr. Mancini. There is no way in Hell that I'm going to sit across from your sister and eat my lunch wearing fucking love eggs." I finish buckling my red stilettos, moving to stand chest to chest with Marco and staring into those steel-gray orbs full of mischief.

"That's the third time today... so absolutely yes, Mrs. Fox-Mancini. But I'm flexible; you could always wear the butt-plug." His grin grows wider as one hand wraps around my waist, pulling me impossibly closer to his body before pushing a hand down my pants.

"Am I fuck—"

"Four. Your pussy doesn't lie. So fucking wet."

Closing my eyes at the sensations as he strokes his fingers over my clit, dipping one inside me, I allow a moan of pleasure to escape.

"Good girl." He breathes the words over my mouth, his breath tickling my lips before he devours me. Then he pushes my pants down and breaks away from me, lowering to his knees. Removing his fingers from my pussy, he pushes my panties further aside to give him better access to slide his tongue over my clit, making my legs shake in anticipation.

"Fuck." I'm so close to coming all over his face, and he's lapping me up as if he hasn't eaten in weeks.

Just as my clit starts to throb, he pushes two tiny balls inside me, and it hits me. This man has beaten every record for getting me off, and my body vibrates with the intensity.

It takes me a moment to regain my senses and I shake my head in defeat, a smile playing on my lips as Marco licks me clean before pushing my panties back in place.

"You're incorrigible."

Marco's response is a growl into my neck after kissing his way back up my body. He pulls my pants up on his way, leaving the love eggs inside me.

"I have some business or I'd be coming with you, this is the next best thing. You can think of all the ways I'm going to fuck you tonight every time the balls move." He licks the fingers he just had inside my pussy, reveling in the taste as he winks down at me.

Well, this lunch date is going to be interesting.

"Does Enzo not want to sit with us?" Putting my fork down, I lean back in my chair and rub my full stomach, trying to contain my flinch as the balls inside me move with my body.

"He's in security mode since everything that happened with Papà. Which means he needs to be a ghost, apparently. Appearing to not be with me, while being with me all at the same time. Honestly, I'm not sure how I'm going to lose him or his goons for my next shift at the club. He's doubled down on everything."

"He's not being much of a ghost today. It's a little hard to miss the giant, brooding Italian man sitting by himself and staring daggers at anyone who comes near us, including the poor waiter."

Lina sips at her water with a frown on her lips.

"He's being a grump lately."

Putting her water down, she rests her arms on the table in front of us and leans forward.

"I know he's grieving too, but it was my fucking dad, you know? It's just hard. And not in the fun way…"

"Alright, Treacle?"

"Oh my God, what the actual fuck? Are you following me or something?" Enzo is immediately up and out of his chair, stalking over to our table with a death glare pinned on the guy in chef's whites, his hand at the small of his back. So much for being a ghost.

I watch the way he takes her in, lustfully, and with a huge smile on his handsome face, and I know. This guy is hot for her. But judging from her reaction, I'm getting asshole vibes.

"I should be askin' you the same thing, Sweetheart. This is my restaurant."

His accent surprises me, but it also suits him. It's a lot like the guys from that *Snatch* movie Ev made me watch a couple of years ago.

"Woah, big guy. What's your deal?" The way he addresses Enzo makes me raise a brow in surprise. This dude clearly has a screw loose. Can he not read the danger coming off of Enzo?

It's kinda hot.

Lina moves to put a hand on Enzo's chest, telling him with her eyes to stand down. He visibly relaxes, stepping back with a gentle kiss to Lina's forehead, and just as I think it's all over and I can put my metaphorical popcorn away, the guy's whole fun-loving attitude changes.

"Is he the reason you wouldn't give me a lap dance?"

Oh Hell, shit's about to go down.

Enzo is barely held back by an exasperated Lina, rolling her eyes as she answers. "Thanks, asshole."

"What did I do?"

"Just say the word, Lina, and I'll make this asshole disappear."

"Ooh, big man, are ya, mate? Got that whole gangster thing goin' for ya. I can dig that."

I love Marco's Italian accent, and he may be a douche, but this guy's cockney accent is a contender for panty-melting trophies.

"Will you fucking stop? Please. Enzo, it's fine, we'll talk later, okay?"

"Damn straight we will." He nods and turns to walk back to his seat, but not before the fucking chef pipes up again.

"Aw, puppy's been told off by Mistress. Go on, big guy, tail between ya legs an' everythin'."

Well, I don't think this restaurant is going to last very long. Enzo must have the strength of a thousand men as he continues to his table without shooting the guy in the head.

"The name's Quinn, Devon Quinn." He holds out his hand for me to shake, and I do, with a small smile playing on my lips. This guy's trying to impress 'the friend' to get the girl.

"I don't care what your name is. And who introduces themself like that anyways? You're not fucking James Bond." His attention is on Lina as she speaks, taking in every word but not actually listening.

"Come on, Darlin'. Gimme one date? Let me show you I'm not a bad guy."

A different waiter than the one who's been serving us chooses that moment to come by to clear our empty plates, placing the bill in the center of the table.

"Oh, fuck no. You ain't paying for shit." Devon goes to grab the bill, but I get there first.

I don't want Lina to owe this guy anything. I don't know him or his intentions. When I'm with Lina, I'm not just her friend, I'm her big sister too, and I look after my family in every way possible.

The little black folder is in my hands before Devon gets to it, and I quirk a brow at him as he looks at me with an amused grin on his face.

"You're a feisty one too, aren't ya?"

"Back off, Bond. You wouldn't know feisty if it bit you in the ass."

Lina's staring at him with curiosity, and I think I know that look. She's interested. *How many men does she need?* Lucky bitch.

I've only got one and I'm exhausted.

Shaking my head at them both, I open the little black book the bill came in. There's a bright red envelope inside, with a similar single red rose as the one I received in my office, thorns and all, and I smile. Marco can't just let me remember him from these damn love eggs in my pussy. I've got to say, this being the second little love note from him is kinda sweet.

I put the bill down, along with my card, and look Devon in the eye. "Have someone charge my card, please. Everything was delicious." He looks skeptical, but I raise a brow at him to let him know I'm serious.

With a mischievous grin, he salutes me and gives Lina a flirtatious wink before walking away. Without my card.

Rolling my eyes, I go to open the red envelope.

"Ooh, who's that from?" Lina leans across the table, eyeing the envelope with curiosity.

I don't respond, a lump in my throat and my heart in my stomach as I take in what the note says. It's not from Marco, at least I know that now, and it makes me sick that I even thought it could be.

*Not long now, Skittles.*

# Chapter Eight

## MARCO

My father always said, "Your gut is your barometer. That constant low-pressure you feel means rain is coming, but instead of getting you wet, it gets you dead."

It's here right now—that pressure—sitting low in my gut, telling me to prepare myself. Telling me that my father's death is bigger than my grief. His death is the open door to big egos and narrow world views, and I'm the only thing standing between them and their ambitions.

"Sir, everyone has arrived. They're in the conference room, as requested." André steps inside and places eight folders on my desk; one for each of the people sitting around that table down the hall. I've met them all, have known them for years, but it doesn't stop me from picking up the files and nodding to my assistant.

"Thank you, I'll be right there." Four capos and four of their best soldiers are waiting to know who will be their next underboss as I take over my father's kingdom. Like them, I went up the ranks. I learned the business my father and his best friend, Stefano, built, one real-estate purchase at a time. This business keeps order in the city, all the while perpetuating chaos, because balance is the only way to keep the peace.

Today, I'm no longer a capo, nor the underboss. Today, I am my father. Even though my father had stepped back on the business side, he was still the proverbial boss. Now I am, officially, the don of the Mancini family. Groomed since the day I was born to be in this position, yet nothing, not a fucking thing, prepared me to step into my father's shoes. The business? Sure. The grief? Not a chance.

But this is no longer about me. This is about my people needing someone to guide them, and it's my responsibility to, in this time of pain for all of us, ensure equilibrium is maintained.

Scanning the folders doesn't teach me more than I already know, but it does refresh my memory about certain qualities and downfalls of each of my employees. Thankfully, my choice for the next underboss hasn't budged.

As soon as I walk in, everyone stands—including Enzo—to show their respect, but I wave them back down as I let the folders in my hands slap onto the cherry oak table built to seat more than twenty people.

"*Buongiorno a tutti*. The coffee and biscotti are for you." My father always had the same spread on the table when meeting with the capos, I figured I'd follow the tradition.

It's late morning, and tonight I'm heading out to Staten Island to meet River, to spend an evening on her turf and enjoy her genuine smiles and ridiculous jokes I love so much. In fact, I love them to the point I'd suffer an evening with her loser ex and his psychotic wife.

*Match made in Hell.*

There are four capos at the table, paired with their number one soldiers, here at my request. It's tradition in our family to announce the next underboss to all four heads, their second-in-command officially becoming a capo him or herself. Contrary to past families, we're not sexist assholes.

I watch them all intently as they talk, some laughing and making big hand gestures, others sitting back and nodding at the right times with guarded eyes.

Each capo heads a specialty, leading thirty to fifty soldiers depending on the need. We own New York City, no other family dares come for us, but we have strict rules about the kind of business we do. If you don't follow those rules to the letter, you don't see another day. It's just the way it goes.

"I know you are all very impatient to hear about my decision, so I'm not going to make you wait much longer."

Enzo—whose only thought is always about my safety—refused to take the underboss seat when I proposed he step up. I figured he'd want the freedom, but he requested to stay exactly where he is. And by 'requested,' I mean he flat out laughed in my face and told me to find someone else. As much as I'd love to think it's because he can't get enough of the drama in my life, I'm pretty sure it has to do with Lina.

"Ray." I pin my current capo who deals with extortion, keeping shops safe from any big city dangers, and watch as he quickly understands what I'm about to tell him. "You've been with us for a long time, your loyalty over the last thirty years has earned you a seat at the head of the table. My father would be happy with this decision."

"*Grazie.*" Ray "The Stinger" Martino's jaw is tense and his hands are clenched, but I'm not worried. He's happy and trying really fucking hard not to show any emotions. "George will be taking my place as capo." He then pins me with his own gaze and adds, "He's proven very valuable, I put my hand to the knife for him."

I look at George, making sure he knows I will end him if he ever thinks of betraying any of us. The silence around the table is uncomfortable for some, I'm sure, but I drink from the cup of ease, knowing it's the exact ingredient that keeps this entire organization alive.

My approval comes in the form of a grunt, giving the members around the table permission to congratulate and shake hands. All, of course, except J "The Shadow," who is the capo of The Reapers.

Few people know who she is, choosing to keep her identity on the down-low since—according to her—it's easier to kill someone when they have no idea you're behind them, let alone capable of slashing their throat with a flick of your wrist.

André steps inside the room and serves a celebratory glass of rich, amber cognac to each of us, and as the last of us is served, we all stand and extend our hand to the middle of the table.

"*Salute.*" The single word echoes around the room as we all bring the glasses to our lips and savor the honeyed splash of exotic fruit across our tongues. On days like these, we don't congratulate with cheap liquor, we show respect with the best this world has to offer.

As we sit back down, I let the silence descend before I begin speaking again.

"Order and control…" I give a little dramatic pause to make sure everyone's attention is solely on me. "It's the only way to keep the business and our families safe." I turn to Tommy, who is aptly nicknamed "Baby Face" and point my index finger at him. "I don't want drugs anywhere near schools in our neighborhoods. If the adult one percent of this city wants to paint their noses in white powder, that's their problem. Children are innocent and we keep them that way. Are we clear?" Tommy nods, determination in his eyes. My attention turns now to George and his new responsibilities. "We don't take money from shops for nothing and we don't force them either. We do business. We offer, not force, protection. If I hear a mom-and-pop store getting a beat down for not accepting our help, I will fucking end you." George, whose receding hairline is far enough back to be considered bald, keeps eye contact with me as he agrees to my terms.

"Sure thing, Boss."

I don't address J because she doesn't need reminding of her job. Not a single member of her team has even veered in the wrong direction. She's been with us for about six years, started out a soldier at the tender age of sixteen when her entire family was murdered in front of her. Instead of going into the system, she headed straight for a made man—just like her father—and told him she was joining the ranks. Six months later, she avenged her parents with her first kill. Few people know her name, which is the only reason she's still alive.

I turn to Eddy "Snake Eyes" Borelli, his mouth set in a permanent sneer due to a beat down from the Bronx police. They had nothing on him and he never spoke a single word.

*Omertà*—the law of silence—is a way of life. And sometimes, death.

"The casinos need to be cleaned up. I've heard shit I don't want to hear. Check the loyalty and discard the weak links." Eddy slowly closes his eyes and bends his head in guise of an answer. He'll get the job done, I have no doubts.

It's not these people I'm worried about. It's some of the hothead soldiers with big egos and small dicks. They're the most dangerous of all.

"Boss?" My eyes shift to J, trying to hold back my surprise. "I took care of a possible breach two days ago." This gets my attention. A breach in her ranks is some serious shit.

"Okay." I steeple my hands at my mouth, my jaw ticking with the need to control everything under me.

"Remember that job in Rose Hill?"

*Fuck.*

"Yeah, what about it?" I can sense Enzo stiffening, his adrenaline rushing through his blood, but I stay calm and stoic.

"I found out one of the clean-up crew was getting a little too friendly with outsiders."

"Who? Who was he talking to?" Enzo voices what I want to ask just as my phone vibrates and I see River's name pop up on the screen. I don't give a fuck what we're talking about. When my wife calls, I answer. I stand and silently tell Enzo to take care of the situation.

Outside the conference room, I answer my call and physically feel my shoulders loosen at the sound of her voice.

"Tesoro."

"Ugh! I forgot the tequila for the Cinco de Mayo celebration." I want to laugh at her dramatics. She sounds like the world stopped rotating because she didn't bring her drug of choice to the party.

"What, do you not have enough weed at your brother's house to keep you happy?" I'm teasing her and she knows it, but she'll still bust my balls, I have no doubt about it.

"Is it too much to ask that you simply say, 'Yes, darling, I'll pick up a couple of bottles before I drive out there'?"

It's way too fucking easy to rile her up.

"Technically, you didn't ask a question." I'm guessing angry sex is on the menu tonight.

"You know what? Forget it. I'll fucking get it myself." I love it when she drops an f-bomb. It means I can turn her luscious ass into a pink spankfest.

"Watch your mouth, Tesoro, or I'll assume you're asking for a punishment."

"I'll ask for divorce papers, how's that?" Three months ago, that threat would have me leaving this meeting and driving out there immediately so I could show her the error of her ways. Today, I just growl in her ear, knowing damn well it soaks her panties and makes her putty in my very capable hands.

"Say that again, Tesoro, and I'll make you swallow every single syllable by fucking your throat like a savage animal." My voice is low, lethal even, and the small moan that escapes through the phone is all I need to know. "Now, be patient. I'll be there soon with enough tequila to keep you happy and my hard dick to keep you satisfied." She's right, I always have to go too far when it comes to her. I can't help it.

"Whatever. Don't forget the lime." That little minx hangs up on me. No one in this fucking city would ever dream about hanging up on me. Hell, just having my number and knowing I would answer her calls at any time, in any place, is a fucking privilege.

Fuck, it's refreshing.

Ten seconds later, as I'm making my way back into the conference room, her name lights up again, freezing me in my spot.

"Did you forget something?"

"Thank you." And she hangs up again.

Progress.

When I walk back inside the room, I have to school my features, wipe the silly schoolboy grin off my face and get back to work.

"So, who was your guy talking to?" Sitting back down, it's now I notice the solemn look on everyone's faces, and the high I was riding from my phone call with River morphs into a pile of bile in my stomach.

"It's bad, Boss. We may have a war on our hands." At his words, I stare at Ray while trying to process this new information.

"The Napolitanos want River."

My head whips to Enzo and my blood boils with rage at his narrowed eyes and ticking jaw.

"Then a war they shall have."

The hotel renovations are on schedule, which is, in and of itself, a feat. But paying a fee that's higher than the asking price usually drives people's motivation.

The meeting with my capos is on a constant loop in my mind, but the different ways to protect River are at the forefront. It's my only priority, if I'm honest, keeping my family safe, but I'm going to need help from those I trust to do so.

A quick glance at my wristwatch tells me it's time to pack up and get my ass to Staten Island, where a very serious and potentially uncomfortable conversation will have to take place with my wife. Any time I ask her to lay low, she tends to do the exact opposite, but this time is different. This time, all bets are off.

"Sir, here are the bottles you requested along with fresh lime." André places the bag on my desk and waits to see if I have any other requests.

"Thank you. Go home and enjoy your weekend. I'll see you on Monday." Bowing his head like he's speaking to royalty—still makes me uneasy—he walks out. I do the same, gathering all I need to work from home if necessary.

As I'm shutting off my computer, there's rustling outside my door and André's voice clearly saying I'm not taking visitors moments before the door swings open wide, and two figures loom over me like a bad mob movie from the fifties.

I lean back in my chair, not bothering to stand and greet the men. Pressing the emergency button under my desk that immediately alarms Enzo, I place my gun at the small of my back, hidden by my jacket.

"Sir, what can I do?" André is in panic mode, but I can't show emotion, it's what these fuckers want and I refuse to give it to them.

"It's fine, André. Go home." I need him to leave and stay safe in case this goes badly. I'm watching the older man, his balding head reflecting the overhead light, a thin sheen of sweat coating it, which tells me he's not as confident as he'd like me to believe.

"Ambrosio, I didn't realize you were in The City." I'm trying to figure out when the fuck this asshole landed on my soil. He's supposed to be in Naples, not on my fucking turf. The problem is that I cannot turn him away, that would be offensive, and I have far too much at stake to show my hand so soon. We are equals in status, but my reach is exponentially larger than his will ever be.

To the outside world, I'm relaxed and in control, but inside, I'm livid. This isn't how we do business. We do not ambush. We do not show up without a courtesy call when stepping into someone else's domain. They are trying to push me into a reaction, but I am a bigger man than that. At least that's what I want them to believe anyway.

"Marco, *come stai*?" Giuseppe Ambrosio enters my office like I imagine a king would walk into his castle. Dressed in a charcoal-gray suit with a crisp white shirt and no tie, he looks every bit the part of the businessman walking into an office to make a deal. His son, Ugo, on the other hand, is still a little punk ass bitch with a chip on his shoulder the size of his ego.

I stand, my hands in my pockets like I don't have a worry in the world. I'm not afraid to die, this job pretty much guarantees a short life span on most days, but I'll be damned if I go down without a brawl.

Giuseppe goes in for an accolade, both hands on either of my shoulders as he leans in and plants a kiss on one cheek then the other. "*Tutte le mie condoglianze per tuo padre*." I doubt this guy flew across the fucking Atlantic Ocean just to express his condolences.

"*Grazie*." My eyes shoot to Ugo, who doesn't pay his respects, only stands there with laser eyes barely hiding his murderous intent like he's just waiting for me to run. Fuck that. I don't run, I fight.

I'm guessing Enzo might take a while before he arrives, given the rush hour traffic on a Friday evening, and I have no doubts this ambush was a calculated move to get me alone and vulnerable.

"You know," Giuseppe walks around my office, looking at the books on my shelf that are mostly about New York City architecture at the turn of the twentieth century, before he cocks his head to the side and stares at me like I'm a puzzle he can't figure out. "I liked you, Marco. Your father and I had plans for this business. A... *come si dice*?" He's looking for a word and I know damn well he's just trying to be dramatic, but I don't have time for these games.

"A partnership?" I offer the word so he can continue his diatribe. I suppose the more he talks the fewer bullets will fly.

"*Si, si*. A partnership, yes." Raising his index finger at me, he shakes it almost in my face like he's trying to scold me. "But you, Marco, did not keep your promise."

Internally, I'm rolling my eyes, because this again?

"Giuseppe, I'm sorry you felt you had to come all the way out here for this, but I never promised to marry your daughter. That was between you and my father and honestly, I don't think Elizabeth wanted to marry me either."

Ugo is now fuming, his nostrils are opening and closing, his mop of dirty blonde hair is sitting on top of his head like it has no place to go except flatly around his skull.

"You sullied her, you son of a bitch."

Wait, I what?

I'm confused and my face must show that something is not computing.

"She's no longer a virgin because of you, Marco, which means none of the Italian families want to take her as a don's wife." Giuseppe's voice is hard now, with a hint of defiance, just waiting for me to call out his daughter as the liar she must be.

There are so many reactions I could have had in that moment, but the only one I'm capable of showing is outright laughter. Green, pissed off laughter that ends with me straightening my back and pinning the Naple's don with my gray eyes.

"I have never slept with Elizabeth, and to be honest, that's beside the point. The old country needs to wake up and smell the misogyny." Fucking Hell, I sound like River and it gives me a little pride.

"We saw you don't care about that since you married a legit whore."

All decorum flies out the window as I reach back, slide out my gun and pin Ugo to the wall with the barrel shoved right under his chin.

"Give me a reason to pull this fucking trigger, Ugo. You wanna come after me? That's fine. Insult my wife, and the only use you will ever be is worm food. *Lo capisci?*" He doesn't answer, so I repeat myself in English this time. "Do. You. Fucking. Understand?" The barrel is digging into his flesh and I know it's going to leave a mark.

"*Calmati*, Marco. We understand, yes. Ugo means no disrespect, right, son?"

I wait for this little fucker to apologize, but he just stares at me with contempt in his eyes. This little shit doesn't give a fuck about his sister, he's pissed he's not at the table, that he's not the new underboss.

I pull the gun away, placing it back behind my waistband, and punch the little shit in the nose, blood erupting like Mount Etna all over my shirt and pants. I'm about to beat his face in when it's my turn to feel the ice-cold steel at the back of my head. Nothing's more frustrating than being held at gunpoint by your own weapon.

"I asked you nicely, Marco." My jaw is tight, my fists are opening and closing with the need to pummel their sorry asses into next year, but I breathe through my rage and turn around, the barrel now flush against my forehead.

"Do it. Kill me, Giuseppe. But before you do, remember this..." I step into his gun, pressing it more firmly into my skin, a demented grin on my face like getting shot is the penultimate gift. "Even with my death, you won't get New York City. Everything is already in place, contingencies are planned out months, years in advance. You and your son can go fuck right off."

Suddenly, the gun is lowered and the fear etched into Guiseppe's aging features tells me he's looking straight into the eyes of the devil.

Enzo must be here. He does love a dramatic entrance.

"There's nothing I would love more than to shoot your son in his pathetic face." A man of few words, but when he speaks, he doesn't play.

"*Bene, bene.* Let's all calm down and have a drink to discuss the future." Giuseppe places the gun on my desk and sits on the couch that's reserved for big investors and quality guests. Of which he is neither.

"Papà! What are you doing?" Elizabeth walks into my office, her eyes darting from my blood-stained shirt to her brother's nose, followed by the gun on the desk. It's pretty obvious that someone almost died tonight. "Come on, let's go. Mamma isn't feeling well, she's asking for you." At this, both father and brother turn their heads to her and stand. I can respect the immediate need to be there for family, but I still want to pummel them.

"Enzo, accompany our guests to the front, please." With a grunt, Enzo leads Giuseppe and Ugo out while Elizabeth stays behind, her cheeks flushed and her breathing shallow, like she ran to get here.

"I'm sorry, Marco. I had no idea they were going to do this."

It's clear I have a situation on my hands. It's also clear that if I don't take care of it, River will be the first one in danger, and that's unacceptable.

"Look, there's a restaurant down the street that everyone is raving about. Let's talk this out and make sure we don't start a war." Elizabeth is now calm and collected, like everything is going to plan.

I watch her, my glare judging her sincerity. No matter what her plan is, I need to keep this city from bloodshed, so I do exactly the opposite of what I want to do. I send River a text message—it's easier than having to explain—telling her I'll be late and to not wait up. Fuck, I hate this.

**Me:** Tesoro, I have an emergency. I'll be late but I'll be there.

**Tesoro:** Is everything okay?

I was expecting snark, so her worry touches me deep in my soul.

**Me:** It will be.

# Chapter Nine
## River

It's been so long since just the four of us were together, wrapped up in blankets surrounding a fire. The heat coming off it keeps us warm and cozy as we toast marshmallows on sticks. Not that we need them. After all the vegetarian Mexican food we've eaten this afternoon, I'm surprised my body isn't protesting.

"I swear I could eat a hundred of these. Baby sure does have a sweet tooth." Petal groans as she finishes off her latest vegan marshmallow, and I smile. Pregnancy looks good on her.

From behind, you'd never know she's pregnant, she's so tiny it's almost impossible to notice. Her stomach has the most perfect little round bump though, and every time Ev is anywhere near her, he strokes his hand protectively over it. I get a sense of pride seeing them like that, and knowing I have a niece or nephew on the way feels really special.

"You sure it's just the baby's sweet tooth, Pet?" Kai laughs from where he's sitting next to Ev as they share a joint. Far enough away from Petal and me that she doesn't inhale the fumes.

"You calling the pregnant woman a liar, Kai?" Petal raises a brow at him in defiance, but her sunshine still shines through, even when she's trying to be serious.

"I would never." Holding his hands up in surrender, Kai winks at her with a smile.

"Didn't think so." She turns her attention to me. "Can you pass over some more marshmallows, please?" Batting her ridiculously long lashes, she grins, tilting her head to the side for added effect, and I can't help but laugh.

"As the official coolest aunt in the world, of course." I pass the bag over to her with a wink, and she stabs at one with her stick, ready to toast the fuck out of it. "Where's Freya tonight?" I don't know why it has just dawned on me that she isn't here, but there you go.

"The treatment she's having is wiping her out a little, so she stayed at home. Only two weeks left to go and she'll be finished. Hopefully, the doc will give her the all clear and we can start moving on." Kai's usual brightness dims as he talks about Freya, and I can only imagine how draining being around her in his own home must be.

She's an energy vampire and I'm glad I'm not the one who has to deal with all of that.

"Has she been staying at your place while you're working in The City?"

"Yeah, her place is further away from Ev and Petal's than mine, and with her parents still off fuck knows where, she wants the support system while I'm working away."

"Fair enough. Ev, wanna roll me one of those and swap places? The lack of tequila today is disappointing." I nudge Petal with my elbow to let her know she's partially to blame for the alcohol drought today. I'm not a huge drinker, and she knows I'm joking, but she's my Cinco de Mayo tequila-buddy.

"Already prepared, Riv." He waves a fresh joint in the air as he stands and we swap seats so he's sitting next to Petal while I plop down on the bean bag closest to Kai. "Are you warm enough, Babe?"

He immediately starts messing around with the blankets, covering Petal's shoulders and all but burying her beneath them. She smiles, and it's clear she doesn't need the warmth he's surrounding her in, but she accepts it all the same, snuggling into him as he finally settles.

"Thanks, Bear." Kissing the top of her head, my baby brother looks so proud and happy with himself and I fucking love that for him.

"Coming to sit in the naughty smoking corner with your bestie?" Kai opens up the blanket he has over himself, gesturing for me to join him underneath it so he can wrap his arms around me like we often do. As much as, for me, it would be a platonic friends thing... I know Kai still has other thoughts and feelings, and I'm not the girl to lead him on if I can help it.

"I am. You can have sharesies if you behave yourself." Laughing, I face him, letting the blanket drape over my knees. I'm also not the girl to drop all my friends—male or female—because of a guy, but I'm aware there are limits.

A streak of hurt flashes across Kai's honey-colored eyes, but it's gone as quickly as it appeared as he holds out a flame for me to light the joint now hanging between my lips.

"The husband not joining us tonight?"

It's a fair question. I literally asked a similar one when enquiring as to where Freya is, but there's something more behind the way he says it. Something I'm absolutely not diving into right now because we're having a nice evening—despite Marco's worrying text just under a couple of hours ago, but he said everything will be okay, and I believe him.

"He will be, he's just running a little late is all." I take a couple of drags on the joint and pass it over, leaning back on my palms and looking to the sky. The stars aren't always visible so close to the big city, but tonight, they're glorious.

"Listen, Riv. I need to tell you something." Kai's voice is a low whisper, our own little bubble of conversation. Much like the one Ev and Petal are having right now as she leans into him and they stare into the sky together. It's fucking pukeworthy, but beautiful all at the same time.

I'm apprehensive about what it is he has to tell me, and I'm not sure if I want to hear it if I'm going by the furrow of his brow. "Oookay. You better pass that back if it's as bad as your face says."

He takes another drag before smiling and handing the joint over to me. "Nah, it might be nothing, I just think you should know."

"Stop dancing around it and tell me then."

With a deep breath, his shoulders sag slightly and he leans forward. "I saw that woman with Marco again. She was going into his hotel and I didn't see her come out again."

"Kai, I love you, but it's not really any of your business. I get that you're looking out for me, and I appreciate it, but no." I hand the joint back to him with a lighthearted wink to hopefully ease the situation and not make it weird. This is the second time Kai's come to me like this, and while I trust Marco, I can't help the doubt that creeps in. "Anyway, how much longer are you working in The City? I'm sure you've told me, but I've slept since then and I can't remember shit right now."

Laughter bubbles up to my throat, desperately wanting to escape, and why the fuck not? Thanks, weed.

"I'm keeping the rest of this for myself, ya little stoner." Kai's trying to keep a straight face, mocking me and my lack of control, but I see the corners of his lips tilting upward so I lightly jab the fucker in the ribs.

My self-defense sessions with Lina and Enzo have been going well, and going by the shock on Kai's face, my jab wasn't as light as I'd anticipated. Whoops?

"Shit, sorry, Kai!" Throwing my hands over my face dramatically, I peek through my fingers at him, relief flooding me when he starts laughing and hands me back the joint.

"Fuck, Riv. I think someone's been a sneaky ninja and had some of those classes we discussed."

"Maybe." I'm nonchalant with my response, having a toke of the joint with a smirk on my lips.

The rumble of Marco's Aston out front jolts me into full awareness, and my muscles finally relax at knowing he's here.

*Fuck... when did I become so obsessed with being around Marco?*

"Sounds like we have company." Petal lifts her head from Everest's lap as she speaks, her eyes growing wider as they look straight past me and she gasps, immediately moving to stand.

I turn, my own eyes widening as I take in Marco's ragged appearance. He has a graze on his cheek, his shirt is covered in blood, and he looks utterly beat. I'm up and rushing over to him as quickly as my legs will carry me, not that I have to go far.

"Fuck, Marco. Are you alright? What happened?" Wrapping my arms around his waist, I pull him closer and rest my head against his chest, being careful in case there are any injuries I can't see.

Holding me tenderly, he gently rubs one palm over my shoulder while the other rests on the back of my head. He inhales into my hair, hopefully taking comfort in whatever it is I can offer him right now. "Tesoro. *Ti amo.*"

He's told me he loves me many times, but I have yet to say it back, and even though I'm pretty sure I really do, now isn't the time for that momentous occasion of finally admitting it out loud.

"Come over by the fire, Marco. Let me help clean you up. Here, River, finish mixing this up into a paste while I clean the blood off his face." Petal hands me a pestle and mortar full of what smells like turmeric and warm water as she takes Marco by the elbow and guides him to where she wants him to sit.

Dread fills me at this situation and I'm a little shell-shocked. On one hand, I never wanted the drama of the life I'm living to affect my family, but Petal's a pro. She's not phased in the slightest as she uses a cloth to gently wipe away the blood covering Marco's face and knuckles—I'm pretty sure it's not all his either. On the other, Marco looks like he's just gone a couple of rounds in the ring with Mike Tyson.

"What the fuck, dude. What happened?" Everest is right next to Petal, his arm over her shoulder as she does her mothering thing. She's built for this shit—mothering, not cleaning blood from someone's face.

Marco sighs, and turns to look at me with pleading eyes, but he obeys as Petal grabs his chin and spins his face back around to her. "I got jumped."

Kai snorts at Marco's words and I glare at him. He shrugs his shoulders unapologetically with a, "What? You believe him?"

"Shut the fuck up, Kai." I continue to grind and smush the paste-like substance as the shock wears off and I sit beside Marco, handing over the pestle and mortar when Petal asks for it.

A thousand things are running through my mind. Did he really get jumped or is it something mafia-based? There isn't anything I can think of, but Marco doesn't exactly discuss the ins and outs of his work, especially not the bits that are illegal or inspire violence.

Petal uses her fingers to smooth the turmeric paste over the graze on Marco's cheek and knuckles while the rest of us stay silent. It's not uncomfortable, but I know it can't stay this way.

"There. Bear, can you take this inside for me, please?" She hands him her tools and he obediently takes them inside the house. "Now, you listen to me, Mister." Petal's voice is barely a whisper as she leans into him, holding his hands in hers, and I strain to hear her words. "A person's aura can say a lot about them. We are a family with no secrets, we've all learned that the hard way. So please, you know what you need to do." Moving back, she looks up at me with a smile. "Go get your husband cleaned up, Riv."

Marco smirks and lightly shakes his head, allowing Petal to hug him before she stands and pulls Kai up from where he was sitting in silence, taking him back into the house with her.

And then there were two.

With his elbows on his knees, Marco rests his head in his hands in some kind of defeat. I move to sit in front of him, resting on my knees, pulling his head into my chest, and brushing my fingers through the long strands of his dark hair.

We don't speak. We just take comfort from each other's presence, and I allow a lone tear to escape my eye at how this man with the world on his shoulders must be feeling right now.

If nothing else, I hope he takes strength from me in this moment. The same strength he has given me when I needed it.

"Are you going to sulk all the way home?"

Marco is wearing one of Everest's White Stripes band T-shirts because he didn't have time to bring spare clothes of his own and well, the white shirt he was wearing last night was burned on the fire. To say he's unhappy about his attire would be an understatement, but I like the casual look on him. Jeans and a T-shirt isn't something I've ever seen him wear.

"I'm not sulking." Keeping his eyes on the road, he adjusts the crotch of the jeans with a frown on his face.

"Okay, well, are we going to talk about what happened last night?" I shift in my seat to look at him properly. I want to see his face as he answers.

There are secrets he's keeping from me that I haven't figured out yet and I'm allowing him to have. Things have been a lot lately, and I don't think either of us have been in a position to be pushed about anything, but going forward, we need to be on the same page.

"I told you, I was jumped on the way to the car."

Hmm, partial truth, but not the whole truth. The way he's tensing his jaw tells me as much.

"Was that the emergency? That you got jumped?"

"No. I had some business that couldn't wait." His grip on the steering wheel tightens, whitening his cut-up knuckles.

"And what was that business?" I take a deep breath, readying myself for answers I probably won't like, but if I'm going to be all in with this man, I need to know. If I don't, then I'm unable to protect my family properly, and that includes Marco now.

"It's nothing for you to worry about, Tesoro." His tone is low, barely audible as he tries to brush off the conversation.

Not to-mother-fucking-day, Mr. Mancini.

"Don't you *Tesoro* me, husband of mine." A low growl comes from his throat as he glances at me. Only briefly, but I see it, the glint in his eye at me calling him my husband. "Don't think that sexy-ass growl will make this conversation end either, asshole." I watch his eyebrow rise in amusement. "Listen, you have to talk to me about things. You promised me that we were a partnership, that you wanted me to stand beside you in all things. And here I am, standing behind you, being left in the dark. I understand you're grieving for your dad, you've had a lot going on, and I know you've got a lot of responsibilities, but you need to let me in. Fully. Not this half-hearted shit, letting me have a say in the charities being helped and all the sunshine and roses crap. Whatever is going on, it's clearly dangerous. And yes, I know I've brought enough danger to our doors already, but even that has something to do with whatever the fuck you're keeping from me. So. Get the fuck over whatever you need to. And let. Me. In. Goddammit, Mancini." My breaths are coming hard and fast now after my little tirade, but it needed to be said.

I'm not a wallflower.

"Fuck, you're hot when you're angry."

It's now I realize that we're no longer moving, Marco has pulled the car over into a little side road surrounded by trees. Not conspicuous at all...

His focus is on me as he unclips his seatbelt, followed by mine.

"Nah-uh. Nope. You're not doing that. Talk to me. Tell me what's going on."

"Are you sure?" A mischievous grin grows on his stupidly perfect face, but I can still see the darkness behind his eyes.

"Marco." My tone is firm, demanding.

"River."

Asshole is mimicking me, trying to do his dickmatizing thing and distract me from the subject at hand.

"Marco." I raise my eyebrows and make my voice sharper to ensure the seriousness of what I'm trying to say.

"River."

Oh my fucking good God, this man will be the death of me. Or I the death of him. Shame, too, I'd miss that talented cock of his.

"Fuck this. When you're ready to have this conversation, come and find me." I climb out of the car, slamming the door behind me, and apologizing to it in my head for the rough treatment, before stomping off back in the direction of Ev and Petal's house.

The calf-length midi-dress I'm wearing with my Timbs isn't the best outfit for a long-ish walk, the skin-hugging material means I have to take shorter steps, but I know I won't have to go far before Marco stops me. I could see it in his eyes. He wants to open up to me, but he's struggling. Walking away may not be the most mature way to deal with it and get what I want, but he needs to know I won't be sexed into oblivion and pretend nothing's going on.

It's not a shock when his hands grip my waist, pulling me into his hard body, and I feel his warm breath at my ear. "I'm sorry, Tesoro."

*Holy fuck, did the great Mancini just apologize?*

"I owe you answers, but not now. Okay? Can it wait until we get home?" He's pleading with me, leaning down and resting his chin on my shoulder. It's sweet as fuck, but he sounds sincere, which is exactly what I wanted. So I concede.

"Fine. But I'm holding you to that. Being a man of your word and all."

"Fair enough. Now walk back to the car, shaking that fine ass of yours, lift up your dress, and put your hands on the hood." He nips at my ear and slaps my ass to get me moving.

Asshole.

Resting my hands on my hips, I turn to look at him with a raised brow. He needs this, and maybe it'll chip away at the darkness in his gaze that has been there since last night.

However, we're a partnership, and it's about time he realized that. So this is my show, not his.

"Why don't *you* walk back to the car, shaking *your* fine ass, drop *your* pants and rest *your* hands on the hood?"

That cheeky glint I love to see in his eyes appears at my demands and he tilts his head in amused acknowledgement before moving over to the car...putting a lot of swing in his hips as he does. I laugh, because it's just too funny not to.

The fact that he's allowing me to take charge this time isn't lost on me. It's a step forward, and one I may need to take advantage of when the mood strikes me. I am, after all, fully experienced in being the dominant in these situations.

Leaning against the car, his zipper open, his hands resting back on the hood, he looks expectantly at me, waiting for whatever I plan to do next. But now that I'm thinking about it, I can't exactly climb him like a tree against the car, because well, I don't want to dent it.

Fuck it, I'll make it work. Marco is a sexy-ass mother fucker with the morning sun slipping through the trees, and despite all the shit, I'm a lucky woman.

I stride over to him with all the confidence in the world and drop to my knees, grasping Marco's already-hard dick in my palm and gently tugging on it. He groans as I begin to lick from his balls to his tip, sucking him into my mouth like the best lollipop in the world. I begin to roll his balls in the palm of my hand, while the other grips his shaft as I continue to suck him off.

Marco moves a hand to my head, trying to control my movements, so I stop and glare up at him with a disapproving look. I allow his cock to pop out of my mouth, with a final suck because it's too good not to, before standing in front of him.

"I didn't tell you to touch my head, Mr. Mancini. Put your back against the tree over there."

"As you wish." He bares his teeth as he heads over to the tree, but I can see the frustration that having no control is giving him. He's fighting his urges, for me, and that makes me feel powerful as all Hell. I'll play with him a little longer before giving him what he wants, though.

I'm wet as fuck right now in anticipation, because every time with this man is fucking amazing.

He stands, waiting for me, his rock-hard cock standing to attention for my viewing pleasure as I slowly stalk toward him.

I lift the skirt of my dress up to my waist as I move, then slide my hands up and over my breasts, tweaking at my covered nipples. Marco lets loose a growl of pleasure, the sight clearly pleasing him as pre-cum leaks from his tip.

"On your knees." I'm standing in front of him now, zero panties in sight because Marco has stolen so many pairs that I refuse to wear them anymore.

Doing as I asked, he eagerly drops to his knees and immediately begins sucking on my clit, grabbing my ass in both hands and squeezing, hard, which is sure to leave bruises. But they are bruises I will cherish.

Oh, fuck, he's good. Going down on me is almost like his superpower and I hold onto his head to keep my knees from buckling at the onslaught from his tongue. One hand moves from my ass, sliding around to my pussy, where he pushes two fingers inside me, hooking them in that way that makes girls go fucking stupid, and the building tsunami inside me explodes into a thousand waterfalls with the sheer force of my orgasm.

I'm practically sitting on his head as he laps up my cum, and I want to hand all control back over to him at this point because I need more of him. All of him.

"Fuck, Marco."

"As you wish, Tesoro." His signature smirk is back on his face as he stands, quickly claiming my lips with his own, forcing me to taste myself on him. I don't know why it's so hot, but suddenly it's like my orgasm never happened and my body is in need of him all over again.

His tongue explores my mouth as much as mine explores his, and we work together, building up a frenzy of sexual need as we grind against each other.

"Back against the tree." I manage to speak in ragged breaths between nips and licks, urging him to do this last thing I ask. I need him inside me, and I need it now.

He moves, taking me with him as he backs up. As soon as he stops, I jump, giving him no warning, but he handles me like a pro, adjusting himself to line up against my pussy as I keep my hands hooked around his neck. Feeling his tip against me, I push myself onto him and groan at the satisfaction of being filled up.

"Oh, God."

"Not God, Tesoro. Your husband," he growls into my mouth as he grips my ass, helping my movements as I ride him hard against the tree.

My pebbled nipples rub against the fabric of my clothes as my clit grinds against the man sliding in and out of me and he circles my asshole with his finger. I'm about to explode once more from the overwhelming sensations he's stirring within me, but I refuse. I want us to come at the same time, feel him throbbing deep inside me as we hit that climax together.

We continue to attack each other's mouths and necks, nipping, sucking, biting, fucking each other like wild animals, and the tingle I love so much with this man begins in my toes, literally curling them as he spins us around so my back is now against the tree. He thrusts into me, again and again, and as his finger pushes into my ass hole and he grunts into my mouth, I let go.

My orgasm is sudden and overpowering, but the pulsating jolts of Marco's cock emptying inside me reminds me that he always knows exactly what I want. And right then, I needed him to follow my lead. Who knew that the man I met months ago, to whom claiming control was the most essential thing in his life, would hand it over to me just because I asked?

I guess love really does change a man.

There is a lot less tension in the air for the rest of the journey home. *Apparently, I'm referring to Marco's as my home now...*

I've got secrets to find out and things to learn as soon as we step inside, because I'm not letting Marco get away with his usual antics by not telling me important shit.

We pull up outside the house, and Stefano is already there, waiting by the curb to go and park the Aston wherever the fuck it gets parked—because it isn't directly outside the house, and there is no garage. Marco usually drops me off and parks it himself, but I'm assuming, with the conversation he knows we're about to have, he's proving that he's not about to run away from this.

Something catches my eye on the floor by the front door as Marco and Stefano whisper between themselves in Italian. One of these days, I'm going to learn the language, then there will be no more secret conversations.

Bending down by the front steps, I lift the brick—why there's even a brick here is beyond me, but whatever—and my stomach drops.

There's an envelope. A red envelope. Decorated the same as the other notes I've had. And while, after the first one, I thought they were the calling card of my husband leaving me love notes, I couldn't have been more wrong.

"Er, Marco..." My voice is shaky, and I'm sure he can sense it in my tone as he immediately stops talking and turns to me.

I hold up the envelope for him to see.

"Ah, fuck."

# Chapter Ten

## Marco

"R enovations look good."

I'm watching the men working on the new security system I insisted we set up at Rapture after River finally told me about the mysterious letters.

*Skittles.*

I know who they're *not* from, considering the usual suspect is dead and buried somewhere not even wild dogs could find him. The cold sweat that ran down my spine when I read the notes was enough to keep me up all night worrying, which is a new reality for me. My entire life has been about finding my enemies and crushing them. The monsters in my world are always visible, as eager for bloodshed as we are. But this? This isn't the same thing.

I don't fucking know who's stalking my wife. Again. The Ambrosios clearly have it out for her, but I can't imagine they had the kind of intel about what went down between Nate and River to pull this stunt. I mean, how the fuck would they know his nickname for her?

"A compliment, that's two in a month. Should I be afraid you're catching feelings?" My tone is rather playful—this is Enzo, after all—but those words in my mouth are like acid melting my brain with the horrid visual of any man trying to steal her away.

"Reel it in, Cujo. Don't be fucking ridiculous." Jesus fucking Christ, I must be tired if I'm letting anyone speak to me this way, even Enzo. He's dedicated his entire life to our family. Hell, I'd say he *is* family, but then that would be awkward for Lina and whatever relationship they're brewing. "All I'm saying is that she placed her money well."

"She did, and I had to break a fucking sweat for her to accept some help." When she renovated Rapture, she wanted to get a loan for a few extra costs she had envisioned.

"I'm sure that conversation went over well." Enzo chuckles beside me, probably thinking about how fucking stubborn River can be when it comes to her independence. I think, somewhere in the back of her mind, she believes she'll end up alone again, which means she doesn't want to be dependent upon anyone or anything. I gave her my word that I wouldn't go anywhere without her, ever, but we both know that in my world, that's a dangerous promise to make.

"Who said it was a conversation?" I start to walk away after that, Enzo's knowing chuckle following me as we make our way across the main floor, eyes scanning the camera angles and making sure the employee doors have new badge scanners.

I grin at the memory of me fucking my wife into submission with her legs wrapped around my neck, her work heels digging into my shoulder blades while her deliciously filthy mouth screamed every obscenity into the space around us.

I let her come only once she agreed to take my money and forget about using a fucking bank.

"Your sister would have my balls if I tried half the shit you do with River." I stop, turn to face him, and scowl.

"I'd have your balls if you tried *any* of the shit I do with River." As soon as the words leave my mouth I hear the overwhelming hypocrisy of my statement. Thankfully, Enzo doesn't call me out.

Well, except for the smirk and raised brow. *Fucker*.

Time to change the fucking subject.

"Any news on the notes? Fingerprints, DNA, fucking anything?" Anyone watching us would think we're having a casual conversation about the weather, or maybe about the color schemes of the club, but my pulse is racing, my nerves are on high alert, and my anger is rising with every second that we don't find these fuckers.

"Not yet. Stefano doesn't have anything on the envelope or paper. I'm guessing whoever it is used gloves. There's no stamp, so no saliva." Enzo's words don't reassure me in the least. Quite the opposite, really.

"Clearly, it's not Nate, so who the fuck knows he used to call her Skittles?" I push my hands into the pockets of my slacks and let my head fall back just half an inch, hoping to alleviate the stress at my nape. I hate that shit had to go down like this. Tyler, Nate, and I were tight... like brothers. His loss is something I'll have to carry with me, but I'll be damned if River pays the price of her self-defense.

"Obviously, the team took care of everything where he was concerned. There is the problem of the rogue Reaper, but he's been dealt with. We know he was communicating with the Ambrosios, and the only link to Nate, for now, is Elizabeth getting cozy with his mother. You need to talk to River. Ask her the hard questions about Nate and who they hung out with." My gaze hardens and swings over to my second in command. "Don't look at me like that, man.

You know I'm right and if you'd quit coddling her, you'd realize she's more of an asset than a burden."

My entire body coils as I turn completely to Enzo, my hands in tight fists, my teeth clenched to the point of near pain. "Watch your fucking mouth, Enzo."

"Relax. You keep treating her like a princess—"

"A *queen*."

"A fucking princess or else you'd sit down and lay it all out on the fucking table. That's it. End of story. Fucking final period." I'm speechless. Actually without words with the gall of him. There are reasons I'm keeping her out of the equation.

"I'm trying to protect her, Enzo. That's the end all." Everything I do is for her.

"Bullshit. You're protecting yourself." My brow raised, I'm trying really fucking hard not to make a scene and honestly, I've had enough brawls these past two weeks, I don't need more stitches.

"Didn't realize you had a death wish." There may not be any venom in my tone, but he's one comment shy of losing a tooth.

"Look me in the eye and tell me straight up that you're not afraid of losing her if you tell her everything." We're both staring daggers at each other when my favorite sound in the world tickles my ear.

"Tell me what?" River Fox-Mancini is a little minx.

Enzo nods his hello then walks away.

*Chicken shit.*

Or maybe that's me. Maybe he's right. Maybe I should just play my hand and hope she'll stay at the table for another round.

There's always plan B. I could lock her up and wait until she comes to her senses and realizes that everything I do is for her.

Almost everything.

"Not—" I stop myself short and look down at the woman who has turned my entire existence upside down. "We need to sit down and have a long, painful conversation, but not today and probably not tomorrow." My hand cups her jaw and I pull her close enough to smell her minty breath and subtle perfume. "But we will have our talk. We will lay down every single one of our secrets then." I squeeze her jaw, forcing her to open her mouth just enough for my tongue to circle her parted lips. "You will stay. You will not rush out in a fit of rage. You will not pack a fucking suitcase and leave our home." I bite her bottom lip and suck the flesh into my mouth before whispering. "You can slap me and you can curse me, but at the end of that conversation you will still love me as much as I love you."

The only reason she hasn't said a word, I'm sure, is because her mouth is trapped. If it weren't, she'd be "fucking" this and "fucking" that at me right about now. Planting one last, lingering kiss, I release her jaw and brace myself for her onslaught.

Except, it doesn't come. River just stands there, staring at me with green eyes so bright and... murderous. Yes, that's good old fashioned ire dancing in her eyes. Okay, fine. Let's fucking do this. I'm ready. I've been on the wrong end of a fucking gun barrel, I can handle her anger.

"Fine." She flashes me the fakest smile imaginable then turns and walks away.

"River, get the fuck back over here."

All I get is her perfectly polished middle finger as she catwalks down the center aisle of her club and into her office.

I think that went well.

My phone rings from the inside pocket of my suit jacket just as I walk into my office. Not many people have this number, it's not something I broadcast to the world and Stefano had his tech guys make it unreachable for anyone outside the chosen few.

When I see Tyler's name flash across my screen, I frown. He's as busy as I am with work, life, and trying to run a multi-billion-dollar business. We don't chit chat. If we have time to spend together, it's usually late at night in one of our offices where we can open the decanter and savor a good Old Fashioned in peace and quiet.

We don't call each other for bullshit conversations, which means this is not good.

"Mancini."

"You sound like a mob boss." I chuckle as I sit behind my desk after popping the button to my jacket and lean back in my chair.

"Hello seems too mundane. Plus, it gives people time to hang up if they know they're talking to me." Tyler laughs on the other end, but it's almost forced. I was right... this call won't be good news. "So what's going on, brother? You don't call out of the blue."

"Yeah, you're right. I don't." I'm guessing he covers the phone with one hand since his next words are muffled as he speaks to his secretary, but when he comes back he seems ready to give me the bad news.

"Eleonor called. Many times, in fact. She's been trying to reach you but you're hard to get on the line."

"Eleonor Reed?" André told me she'd tried calling but with so much shit happening, I haven't had the time to sit down and take her call.

"She goes by her maiden name now, but yes, Nate's mom." I nod, even though he can't see me.

"What's so important? Is she okay?" I've had my whole life to practice the necessary nonchalance that goes with my world and my title, but Tyler is too sharp, always has been.

"Nate's missing, she hasn't had any news in over a month. Got a couple of text messages, but then everything stopped." He pauses, waiting for me to tell him I had nothing to do with his disappearance. But here's the thing. Tyler and I don't lie to each other. Nate used to be part of that pact, but he broke our bond when he went off script and tried to hurt River.

"I haven't heard from him either, but he and I weren't exactly on talking terms, you know." All truths. Technically, I'm not lying. No one has heard from him... including myself.

"Right, right. The River thing. How is she, by the way? Are you treating her right?" There's a trace of humor in his tone, like he's goading me, and I know he's about to piss me off before the words even come out of his mouth. "She should have said yes to my offer. She could have everything she has today *and* a good man." I remind myself he's kidding because A: he's dating my sister—I think—and B: River's my wife and I will fucking end him.

"But then she'd be bored out of her mind and cheat on you with me so... you know, she went straight to the happily ever after." It's a low blow, but his ex-wife was a cunt and I'm happy he's over that bitch. I'd offered to make her disappear, but Tyler is too good to be friends with a man like me.

"Seriously, Marco. Call her back, she's freaking out. I am too, if I'm being honest." He doesn't want to ask questions, that's not something we do over the phone and mobile phones are never secure enough.

"Of course, I'll call her right away. Thanks, man."

When we disconnect, I sit and stare at the closed door of my office and think about what, exactly, I'm going to tell Nathaniel's mother. Of course, I know the story we're telling, but I need a moment to remember why we did what we did.

For River. To protect her. Yes, it was in self-defense, but no matter what, I don't need the police sniffing at my door or anywhere near my life, much less her past. Plus, I need to make sure my words don't contradict anything we've said in the past. With Elizabeth staying at Eleonor's house, I'm afraid the Ambrosios are snooping around for intel that could eventually be detrimental to River.

With renewed motivation, I call André through the intercom.

"Sir?"

"Get me Eleonor Reed on the phone, please."

"I don't think she uses the Reed name anymore, sir." I flash him an annoyed glare. Can anyone in my life just do what I say and not give me a fucking etiquette lesson?

"Thank you." My tone is clipped, my calm hanging on by a thin thread, but thankfully André is used to my mood swings.

I barely have three minutes before the line is ringing and the raspy voice of Eleonor Reed answers with urgency. Nope, Eleonor fucking Hunter.

"Marco? Oh, thank God! I've been trying to reach you for days, I'm sick with worry."

Fuck, I'm going to Hell. Growing up, Nate spent most of his time with Tyler and me, saying he liked it better at our place because we didn't have parents constantly screaming at each other. He was right. Tyler's parents are every kid's dream, even though we used to pretend that their overt affection was disgusting, I think we all wished we'd, one day, find exactly that. My parents were loving and always had fun things for us kids to do, but anything beyond that was never displayed to the public.

Nate's parents? Not so much.

"Eleonor, I just spoke to Tyler. Things have been hectic around here, I apologize for the late call back." I hear the wet notes of tears in her voice and, although it pains me, I have to remember that in deceiving her, I'm protecting River and that will always win out.

"I haven't heard a word from Nathaniel in over a month. I was hoping you had some news. Maybe he called you? I know he was upset about you marrying this girl..." I can't help the small growl that escapes my chest and if the gasp on the other end of the phone is any indication, she heard me. "Her name is River and she is my wife, Eleonor."

"Of course, Marco, of course. I didn't mean any disrespect, but I'm a mess. I'm desperate or I wouldn't have bothered you." I let my anger subside a little and remember a mother's love is above all else. At least, that's what my parents have always told me.

"I understand. Unfortunately, Nate and I did, indeed, have a falling out so I'm afraid the last person he would try to contact is me." I pause for effect before handing her the story we planted for the world to believe as to Nate's whereabouts. "Last I heard, he was in Nigeria volunteering for Doctors Without Borders. Is that not the case?" I hear her sniffing so I wait for her to settle a little before adding. "Maybe he's just licking his wounds and as soon as he's feeling better, he'll contact you." He won't because in approximately two weeks, his body will be found somewhere off the shores of Lagos. Like I've always said, I have a guy.

There's a sound, like a snarl, on the other end of the phone, but I must be hallucinating because I can't imagine such a mundane noise coming from someone who has made sophistication her only talent in life.

"Right. You're right. Broken hearts are better healed in the company of strangers." There is zero sincerity to her words, but that's okay. She's in pain, probably already in mourning, and I have to respect that. Yet, something niggles at the back of my mind. I really do not like her tone with me.

"I'm sorry I couldn't be much more help to you, Eleonor. If there's anything I can do for you, let my assistant know and we'll set things up." We won't, but if circumstances were different, I would absolutely offer my help.

"Hmm, thank you, Marco. I'll be sure to let you know." She hangs up. No goodbyes or pleasantries, but again, a mother in mourning deserves understanding.

"Fuck." The only thing that could make this remotely better is having my wife in front of me. Better yet, laid out on my desk like my favorite meal so I could get my fill of vitamin R.

Unfortunately, I need answers first.

It only takes me seconds to get Enzo on the phone.

"We have a problem."

"Be right there."

Some things are better said in person and talking about who fucked up on the Nate cover-up is definitely not something I'll be doing over the phone.

Ten minutes later, he's strutting into my office and dwarfing the seat across the desk from me.

"What's up?"

"Eleonor Reed just called me," I see him about to correct me, but I lift a finger in guise of telling him to shut the fuck up. "I fucking know she goes by her maiden name, asshole, but I just don't care enough to remember it so let it fucking go."

Shrugging, he takes out his phone and goes to his notes, so I continue.

"I thought we had someone texting her on the regular? A couple of phone calls with bad reception? I thought you took care of this, Enzo…" My tone is a bit harsh, but this shit should have been tight.

"I did. The Reapers always get shit done." His fingers are flying across his phone and I'm guessing he's setting up a meeting with J.

"Does this have anything to do with what J told us about the breach on her team?" I'm pulling out the files on my capos, stopping when I find "The Shadow" and opening it to the list of soldiers she manages.

"She'll be here in ten." He drops his phone back in his suit jacket pocket, looking straight at me, and I know.

I fucking know I'm about to get really fucking pissed off.

"Someone fucked up."

"Who? I want names right fucking now." My molars are getting a workout and my entire body is shaking with barely restrained anger.

"Our best guess is the kid J caught sniffing around the Ambrosio crew." Now I'm confused.

"I thought that shit was taken care of." I'm looking at the kid's file—and I don't use the word "kid" lightly. He can't be more than twenty years old. Christ, he can barely grow a fucking beard.

"She did, but apparently not before the body disappeared." My head snaps up at his words.

"Define... disappeared." This day is officially complete and utter shit.

"The shipping container in Lagos is empty. We had one of our men open it and check to make sure everything was in place, but Nate's body wasn't there." Enzo barely flinches at this news and it's a good thing, because someone needs to stay clear headed while my entire plan explodes into nothingness.

"So, what you're saying is that Nate's body could wash up on the shores of my fucking city any day now?" Just as I stand, there's one knock on my office door before J walks in and shuts us back inside.

My ire suddenly finds the right victim, but before I have time to lash out, she slaps a folder on my desk and looks me straight in the eyes.

"This guy?" J points to a picture from her folder. "His name is Rafy Gambino. He was tasked with keeping in touch with Eleonor during the job's travels." In his thirties, he's the perfect stereotype of the Italian mafia. Slick, cocky, and high on power.

"And?" I need her to get to the point.

"His body was found this morning." She looks at her watch and shrugs. "Well, technically, last night, in the middle of Piazza del Plebiscito." She waits for me to put all the pieces together, and it's clear to Enzo and me when we do.

"In Naples."

"Yes. Two bullets to the head, but that was after they cut out his tongue. I'm guessing he was tortured for hours before they took mercy on him. No fingernails, missing teeth, and one of his ears was cut off too." I nod at her words, especially the ones she isn't saying.

"It's safe to assume our guy talked. That's why the two bullets. It's not mercy, it's a message." Standing over my desk, I stare at Enzo as he clarifies the Ambrosio family's work ethics and it's clear to us all that shit's about to explode.

War has begun.

"I need you to get River and Lina to the Hamptons on lockdown. I need our best soldiers for security detail to have a look around, making sure the security system there hasn't been tampered with."

History always has a way of repeating itself.

The greatest wars of our civilization have been fought in the name of the women we love.

# Chapter Eleven
## River

Twenty days.

Twenty mother fucking days since I was promised answers, and Marco's still keeping some big-ass secrets from me.

Admittedly, having another red envelope addressed to me showing up on the literal doorstep has set some new balls in motion. Not the fun kind of balls either. It's just given Marco excuses to have the conversation I'm craving when he "has more information" because he doesn't want to worry me.

Total crock of shit to be honest because I'm only worrying more with the not knowing, but I've allowed it... allowed him to believe I'm accepting his silence.

Little does he know, I've got my own *people*. A network of escorts can find out almost anything in this city, so I had Sheryl arrange a meeting with our most loyal girls—and guys, I figured adding guys to the roster would be a winner, and it is.

Now, it's just a waiting game.

One that involves spending time in the Hamptons. Marco's mom was finally ready to come home. At least, that's the reason I've been given, and while I believe it—to some extent—I know it has something to do with the notes as well. They scared the shit out of me, left a lump of lead in my stomach, and this is exactly why I'm not fighting him on this trip. I'm not fucking stupid.

It's not the first time I've had a stalker of some kind, but it is the first time I've had someone to support me and help keep me safe.

My mind is currently a fucked up, self-contradicting mess. There is no getting over the things I've been through. The pain and sadness doesn't disappear, but I'm a badass bitch who's learning to grow around all that, learning to make the happy bigger than the sad.

Leaning into Marco, the sand beneath my bare feet as they sit just off the blanket, I let out a soft sigh of contentment. Here, in this moment, the shit all seems miniscule.

"What's on your mind, Tesoro?" He moves his arm up and around my shoulder, stroking up and down my arm as he plants a gentle kiss on the top of my head.

"I don't think you're ready for that conversation yet." I shift and smirk up at him, receiving an eye roll in response. "Well, you asked." Relaxing my head back in its original position against his chest, I smile. Even Marco's annoying eye roll is sexy, and I know there are secrets between us—which I hate with a passion—but I also know they're not being kept maliciously. This man would do anything for me, which makes me a very lucky lady, indeed.

Listening to the beat of Marco's heart, I watch as the sea meets the sand, sliding seamlessly across it with the rhythm of the waves. The sun is creeping beneath the horizon, causing the sky to shine in glorious deep oranges, and I spot my first evening runner jogging along the beach.

That is some dedication to fitness right there. Either that, or this person is exorcising their demons by punishing their body. Because, to me, going for a jog is absolutely a punishment. I'd rather slay my demons in other ways. One of those being with my husband.

I allow my hand to creep up Marco's thigh, my fingers dancing across his bare skin and up to his stomach as I slowly lift his black T-shirt.

"You keep doing that and we're both going to get sand everywhere." His words are a low growl, just how I like it.

The sound has a direct link to my clit, and I look up at him, smiling with mischievous thoughts.

His gray eyes are alight with passion and lust and pure love for me, and I damn near melt under his gaze. We could be seen out here by anyone and that thought sends a whole other kind of thrill through my body.

Gripping the bottom of his T-shirt, I tug at it so he lifts his arms, which he willingly does with a huge smirk on his gorgeous face. Once it's off, he leans back on his hands, his legs sprawled out in front of him, and the eye contact is intense and sexy as Hell. I straddle him, the short red skater-style dress I'm wearing making it easy to split my legs over his muscled thighs.

"I think we're about to get sand everywhere, Mr. Mancini. Can you handle that?"

He raises a brow in amusement as I rest my hands against his chest and place soft kisses across his collarbone and neck, growling when I reach his pulse points and nip gently.

"The question, Tesoro, is can *you* handle it?" He reaches between us to free his throbbing cock from its restraints—because yes, underwear is restraining, which is why I'm not wearing any.

I'm already wet just from rubbing myself against him and he can feel it with his hand between us as he places his tip at my entrance.

"You're a filthy girl. No panties again and dripping wet for me." In what feels like one movement, he grabs my ass and thrusts into my pussy, leaning forward to pull the top of my dress down with his other hand and sucking my nipple into his mouth. He bites and flicks his tongue against it and I'm mewling from the attention.

I swear, I've been close to one of those illusive nipple-only orgasms with this man. He's a fucking genius with his teeth and tongue.

I bounce up and down, riding his giant penis like it's giving me oxygen, my head thrown back in ecstasy as he continues to grip my ass and suck my nipples.

"Don't come until I give you permission."

What the fuck? I'm so close. I kind of want to disobey him, just to see what punishment I'll get, but he must sense it because he slaps my ass and says, "No," before attacking my mouth with the same vigor he gave my nipples.

I moan into him, and he responds with a groan of his own, sending delicious vibrations throughout my whole body, and I have to concentrate really hard not to come.

He moves his mouth back to my rock-hard nipples at the same time as the tip of his finger presses against my ass hole. If he goes any further, I'm sure to explode. I speed up my movements, riding him harder, feeling him deeper inside me, and I hope to fuck he's close.

"Now, Tesoro."

Oh, thank you, gods… or should I say, *husband*…?

I scream with my release, my clit rubbing against him, his finger in my ass, his mouth on my nipple, and his cock so deep inside me it could come back up my throat. He comes at the same time, coating my insides with a few final pumps as he pops my nipple out of his mouth and claims my lips in a searing kiss.

"If you had panties I could clean you up with them. Dirty girl." His smirk says a thousand more words that he doesn't speak, and I shrug as I pick up his discarded T-shirt with a wink.

"It's okay, this will do." Standing, I use his T-shirt to clean up, smirking right back at my smarmy asshole of a husband, and he just laughs. Another clit-tingling sound… everything with Marco causes all these feelings, even when he's pissing me off. It's something I've never experienced before, but it kind of reminds me of Mr. Bobby and his beautiful wife. Gods bless their souls.

"Where'd you go, Tesoro. Are you okay?"

I must have zoned out for a wistful moment, as Marco is now standing behind me, his arms wrapping around my waist, with his chin rested on my shoulder. I'm not about to tell him where my mind wandered off to, I'm not ready, but I know he can read me like a book.

"Yeah. Wanna head back? Your mom said she was making spaghetti for dinner."

His eyes tell me he knows I'm just changing the subject, but he goes with it, holding out his arm for me to take. I make sure my boobs are back inside the dress, scrunching up his T-shirt, wrapping it in the blanket we were sitting on, and moving alongside him back home.

The house is about fifteen minutes from the beach, and there are a few other properties dotted along the way, each one as beautiful as the next. It's not somewhere I'd ever want to build my own home though. My entire adult life was about appearances and status. I've experienced the deceit and lies that come with those things—in many ways—and it's no longer for me.

As we are nearing the end of the beach, a flash of beautiful long red hair catches my attention. No... it can't be. That would be way too big of a coincidence.

It fucking is. And is that...?

Unicorn-pigs must be flying somewhere because I can't believe my eyes.

Kai... with Elizabeth.

"Jesus Fucking Christ." Marco speaks the words that are going through my head out loud and we both pause in equal shock.

"What do you know about this?" I look to Marco, a hand on my hip in question. He's not about to try and tell me he knew nothing. This man knows everything.

"Fuck." He rubs a hand across his forehead before his eyes hold mine in place. "Okay, so I knew Elizabeth had bought a home in the Hamptons, and I recommended Kai to her for the renovations when she asked if I knew anyone."

Oh fucking really?

"Is this what you discussed at your *emergency* dinner with her before you got jumped a few weeks ago?" He didn't keep the dinner a secret from me, said it was some shit to do with keeping the peace with the Naples family, and I believe him, but it doesn't mean it doesn't grate my every last jealous nerve. But I keep it in check—mostly—because I'd expect the same respect when I do things with my friends, like Kai. The fucking traitor.

"Actually, yes. It was discussed."

"Well, okay then." I literally have no more words to say without sounding like a petty little bitch, and that isn't me.

While we've been standing here, Kai and Elizabeth have obviously spotted us and are now heading in our direction.

"Isn't it a small world?" Elizabeth moves in to air kiss us both on the cheeks, and I want to stab her in her stupidly beautiful eyes for even looking at my husband, let alone putting her aura anywhere near him.

Kai looks a little sheepish; he knows what he's done. He's the one who has been telling me about Elizabeth's encounters with Marco—not that I needed telling. He's well aware of the whole Elizabeth situation, yet here he is, probably sleeping with the enemy.

"How far away from here is your place?" Marco's brow is furrowed slightly in curiosity.

"Oh just five minutes from here. Papà surprised me with it and this area is stunning."

Hmm... how fucking convenient.

"Kai, could I have a word?" Marco's grip on my waist tightens slightly and I glare at him, telling him with one look that he needs to let me go.

"Sure."

Marco releases his grip, but not before planting a slightly inappropriate kiss on my lips, which I'm not sorry about... it showed Elizabeth as much as Kai that Marco and I belong to each other.

We move a little further away so we can speak privately.

"What in the actual fuck are you doing with her, Kai? She's a cunt, and you have a wife."

He looks a little taken aback by my brashness, but I'm not pulling any punches with him. It's not something we do with each other.

"It's a job, Riv. One that pays very fucking well."

"Oh, so you're suddenly all about the money? What happened to not working for *the man?*"

I'm not sure what has me so angry about this whole situation. He can obviously do what or who he likes, I just don't feel like Elizabeth is someone he should be getting involved with in any way. I get all kinds of bad vibes from the whole situation and I can't place why.

"If you must know, and I suppose you do because she was your friend once..." He takes a deep, defeated breath before continuing, and now I feel bad for a whole other reason. "Freya's treatments didn't work as well as expected. So she's trying some other things and it's not all covered under my insurance. Okay?"

Fuck, that's not what I was expecting. Now I feel like shit for giving him a hard time. But still... Elizabeth? No.

"I can lend you money if you need it, Kai. You don't need to go back on all your beliefs for her."

"I kind of do, Riv. I agreed to marry her, and while I know it was for all the wrong reasons, I've got to stand by her. She has no one else. And I won't borrow your money, you've done enough for everyone already."

Double fuck. Now *I'm* the cunt.

"Fine. But be fucking careful. She's a snake, and you know damn well I'm not just saying that to be a bitch. You know where I am if you do need anything. I mean it. Whatever you need."

"As do you, Psyche. I'm always going to be here for you. You and me are the forever kind of shit."

A mischievous glint passes through his features, but he schools it quickly, nodding once and holding out his arm to walk me back to Elizabeth and Marco, who are standing around in awkward silence.

I guess we're done here.

After leaving the most awkward encounter on the beach, we finally make it back to the stunning landscaping and architecture that is Marco's mom's home. It's like something out of a magazine, with blankets of greenery surrounding us, from the tall trees and sculptured plants to the expansive, rolling lawns you can't find in The City outside of Central Park.

"I have sand in my unspeakable places. Wanna come help me wash it all out?" I ask as we reach the front door.

"I'll be there in five minutes, Tesoro." I know he wants to go and check on his mom, let her—and Enzo—know he's home.

Marco's bedroom—which is ours now, I guess—is masculine and usually has a strong, calm aura when I walk in, but today, something is off. Though I'm not sure what. Maybe my senses are fucking with me lately, Karma playing her games because I've done some questionable things.

No, it's not that.

My whole body begins to vibrate with anxiety and my breathing starts coming in short, sharp pants as I notice the red envelope on my pillow. *My* pillow, not Marco's...

My vision begins to blur at the edges as I try to control my breathing enough to call for Marco.

Someone has been in this room and that's why it feels off. What if they're still here? My space has been violated yet again. But I'll survive, I always do.

My breathing is beginning to even out as I inhale through my nose and exhale through my mouth, but I'm still curled up on the floor when Marco enters the room, immediately scooping me into his arms and holding me close.

This is the point it hits me, that I now have the resources at my fingertips to execute my own revenge, and I swear to fuck, whoever this is will have a taste of this new version of myself. As much as this stalker feels more threatening somehow, I'm stronger than I was before.

So bring it on, motherfucker.

# Chapter Twelve

## Marco

"What do you say we make a frittata?"

Newspaper in hand and hiding my whole face, I can practically hear the gears turning in my wife's beautiful head as my mother asks her that question. River has no idea about anything Italian; our traditions, our cuisine, and don't get me started on our language. Which, truth be told, is a travesty.

But here's the thing about River Fox-Mancini... she's a quick study. Once she's decided to put her mind into something, she finds a way to integrate it into her knowl-edge base.

Today's lesson is about breakfast and the meal that saves last-minute food from going bad.

"A fri-what-what?" I grin behind the safety of my news-paper as my mother chuckles. It's the happiest I've heard her since my father passed, and that's not saying much. I keep telling her to be herself, that she doesn't have to put on a brave face, but sliding on her don's wife mask is now second nature to her. She and River have a lot in common in that regard.

"A frittata. Come over here, let's do this together."

Eagerly, River slides off her stool where we are propped at the center bar, gently placing Bruce on the floor from where he was perched on her lap. As she walks around to join my mother, she stops next to me and kisses my cheek.

Oh Hell no.

Quick as a viper, my arm shoots out and wraps around her waist just before she runs off out of reach, and I pull her back into my side where she belongs.

"What the Hell was that?" I'm scowling, but from River's smirk, I must not be very convincing.

"Am I not allowed to give my husband a kiss before I learn how to cook fri-something-something?"

"It's frittata. Two t's, one t. Fri-tta-ta." I say it slowly so she can repeat it, but of course she surprises me with her own brand of nutty.

"Oh! Like... Free the tatas. Okay, I can remember that." She's beaming up at me like a kid on Christmas morning, and I don't have the heart to tell her she's not freeing the tatas until she's alone in our bedroom and I can suck on her nipples until she's too weak for her stubbornness.

"Sure, Tesoro. Just like that. Now give me a kiss worth remembering."

Planting both of her hands on either side of my face, River looks me straight in the eyes and whispers just for us, "Everything about you is worth remembering."

It's not quite the words I long to hear from her, but holy fuck, it's close enough.

I'm not worried though. She may not know she loves me, but I do. I love her and I know she feels the same way. As soon as she realizes it, she won't go down easy. I'll have to fuck the confession right out of her and, to be honest, I really don't mind the trouble.

Her mouth traps my bottom lip just as her teeth graze my flesh, pulling hard enough to make me pinch her waist.

"Ow!"

"I think that's my line, Tesoro."

"You're mean." She fake pouts before stepping out of reach and making her way to my patiently waiting mother.

"Says the cannibal." My quip is just that... lighthearted and fun. When the fuck did I become that guy? Enzo's right, her mere presence has given me a partial lobotomy.

"Be nice."

Wow, I thought mothers were supposed to always stick up for their sons.

"Who's not being nice?"

Great, now it's three against one. Maybe it's time for me to change rooms, except that would take me away from River.

"Your brother is calling me names."

"You seemed to like it last night."

"Madelina!"

"Lina!" My mother and River cry out at the same time, and I just raise my newspaper back up and grin like the Cheshire Cat... again, putting my fist out for Lina to bump as she passes me by.

"What? Are we ignoring the fact that these walls are surprisingly thin?"

Now, I love the idea of the entire neighborhood knowing that my wife is satisfied, but there's a line I don't really want to cross and that's here, in the kitchen, with my mother.

"Come, help us with the frittata instead of being silly."

And so it goes for the next ten minutes. The chopping of onions, the washing of peppers, the breaking of eggs, all thrown together like an omelet into the oven.

"What about the *salsiccia*?"

This gets my attention, so I bend a corner of the paper and look at my mother, whose gaze is far away, like she's remembering another life.

"It's probably what killed your father. Too greasy." She places the dish in the oven and when she turns back to us, she's got her brave face back on.

Fuck, I'm too young to give up *salsiccia*.

"Boss, I need to speak with you." Enzo's sudden presence interrupts the cooking lesson. With a wink and a grin aimed at my wife, I follow him out onto the deck where the early June heat has settled for the day.

"What's going on?" My hands in my jeans pockets—being here at the house has taught me the benefits of dressing casually—I watch my second-in-command taking charge of whatever situation we have on our plates.

"We've got a hit on the fingerprints. It wasn't easy getting into the FBI's database, but Stefano's guy is fucking impressive."

I nod, my shoulders squaring, my entire body ready for a fight.

"Then let's do this."

"Long Island?" He's asking me if we're going to our warehouse where our more delicate business takes place.

"Long Island," I confirm, we're going to fuck some people up.

It took a little convincing on my part to leave without River. Not because she's needy, but because she wants to go to The City to check in on her business. I get it. She's the boss now, her employees depend on her to take care of them.

Except who's going to take care of them if she's dead?

Fuck, just the thought makes me nauseous.

"You don't play fair, Marco Mancini." Those were her parting words right before I kissed her hard enough to get her wet and ready for me.

"I'll be back before you know it and then I'll fuck the belligerence right out of you."

"Asshole."

"I can fuck that, too, Tesoro. All you gotta do is ask."

I grin at the memory of our conversation, and of course Enzo notices and can't help giving me shit.

"Not sure that lover-boy's smile is going to intimidate this motherfucker."

"Don't worry about me. Or him for that matter."

He grunts, knowing exactly what I'm planning to do.

The warehouse is nondescript in a shady part of town where we own the three adjacent blocks surrounding it.

Outside, it looks like it's going to ruins, but inside, we set it up for our shipping business on one end and for… interrogations on the other. The floor is slightly slanted toward the middle with a large drain that is regularly cleaned out with hefty amounts of bleach.

We drive my car into one of the open garages that someone closes just as I turn off the engine.

"Tell me about him." I need to know everything I can about this asshole.

"Kevin Moss, twenty-six, only child. Parents are Henry and Heather Moss, living in Atlantic City where Kevin picked up his gambling habit. Owes money, lots of it."

I nod because it's always the same shit.

"Any leverage on the parents?" Sometimes it's easier to get information when you threaten the loved ones more than the actual person being held.

"Nah, working class, no debts but living frugally. They don't spend more than necessary, but Kevin's been living way above his means for some time and now the bank is calling." Enzo snorts like he's making some kind of world-class joke. "Except his bank doesn't repo, they break knees."

Loan sharks, of course.

"Who is it?" Glancing at the center console for the time, I tell myself this needs to be quick. My family is at the beach without me and, granted, they have security fit for the president, I can't stand the idea that I'm not personally there.

"That's what we need to find out. Stefano said it was two punks from the Bronx, but they're not officially affiliated with anyone, which means..." He doesn't want to assume, but I will.

"Ambrosio."

"Ambrosio."

We need to be sure before I turn this city to ash and burn that whole fucking family to the ground.

We exit the car and walk in unison to the open space of the warehouse. It's big enough to host a rave party, yet the only sound this part of town has ever heard are the screams of its victims.

I don't speak as we slowly make our way to the center where a man sits on a chair, his arms secured to the armrests with zip ties so tight I can see his circulation is being restricted just enough to be painful. He turns his head left then right, hearing the sound of our shoes, but with a black bag over his head, he has no idea what's happened to him.

Mostly, he has no idea what's about to happen to him.

"Who is it? Whadd'ya want from me? I don't know nothing about nothing. Please. You got the wrong guy." I look over at Enzo as we read each other's minds. These guys are so fucking predicable. They get mixed up with dangerous people but when it's time to play hard, they pussy out within seconds.

"Kevin Moss?" I confirm his identity for my peace of mind.

"Y-yes. That's me but... I didn't do nothin'." Enzo hands me my favorite knife, with the straight edge on one side and the half-moon hooks on the other. Great for carving and slicing, depending on the situation.

"Been visiting the Hamptons lately?" The only reason I hear his quick inhale is because I was waiting for it. It's a tell-tale sign in these situations. It's obvious he thought he'd gotten away with his little assignment.

Clearly, he failed.

"It's the season, right? Lots of rich, pretty girls up there. Can't blame a guy, right?"

With the tip of my knife, I catch the fabric of his hood and slowly pull it up and over his head. I want to see this fucker's face and watch the very moment he understands his life is worth nothing.

Flicking my wrist, I send the material flying and revel in the sound of his gasp.

That's right, he recognizes me and it's like music to my fucking ears.

"You know who I am?" I cock my head and drag the tip of my knife down the side of his cheek, leaving a thin red line in my wake. It's not a deep cut. Not yet.

"Y-yeah, s-s-sure. You're Ma-Marco Mancini." His voice trembles with every letter he stutters out of his filthy mouth.

"Ah, fuck... I hate it when they piss themselves." Enzo groans at the dripping sound coming from underneath the chair, but his facial expression says he's bored.

"Tell me, Kevin Moss, do I look like a guy who has time to play with his food?" My knife is back at his face, the straight edge digging into his lower lip. "Don't you think I have more important shit to do than to be here listening to your lying mouth." With a flick of my wrist, his lip is cut open and bleeding down all over his chin and neck and clothes. His scream is high-pitched, no doubt he wasn't expecting me to start the game so soon, before I've even asked the first question.

"I don't know whatchu want, Mr. Mancini. I swear it." Speaking is more difficult with half his lip unattached, but I can still understand him.

"Right. Well, let me tell you exactly what I want." Pressing my knife to his lip I watch as he starts crying, his blood mixing with his saliva and his tears. It's a fucking mess, is what it is. "I want to know who sent you to my house. To my bedroom." I lean down so I'm mere inches away from his petrified eyes, my hand fisting his hair so all he can see is me and my barely-controlled rage. "Tell me, when you touched my wife's pillow as you put that note there, did you know you were signing your death warrant?"

Kevin whimpers at my words because he knows. He fucking *knows* I'm going to end him and that I'm going to enjoy every fucking second of it.

"I didn't know whose house it was, I swear it. They gave me an address and a letter. That's it. I swear, I swear." He's sobbing now, his entire face is a goddamn mess. I step back, unwilling to get any of his bodily liquids on me.

"Who gave you the envelope?" Enzo takes over while I walk to the sink set up at the base of the closest pillar to rinse off my knife, but my attention is solely on Kevin's next words. Words that won't save his life, but may save his parents.

"I dunno. I dunno. I got debt, ya know. I was told to do this job and that my debts would be even. I swear, I didn't know. I woulda never have gone to your house willingly, Mr. Mancini. I swear it." If he tells me he swears one more time, I'm going to cut out his tongue.

"Do you believe him, Enzo?" This is our game. Good mob boss, bad mob boss. Except we're both bad and poor Kevin knows it.

"I mean, he's got a convincing way about him."

Kevin's eyes light up with a spark of hope as he nods his head, agreeing with Enzo's bullshit line.

"Hmm, he does, he does. I just need to make sure. You understand, right, Kevin? I have to protect my wife."

Kevin nods more assertively, his lip bleeding all over him, his saliva falling in long dribbles onto his lap.

"So let me ask you this..." I bring the knife to his balls and push just enough to make him whimper. "Do your parents know who gave you the envelope?" Kevin's eyes widen at my question, his fear now real and palpable. I've gone there. I've now threatened his parents without actually saying the words.

"No, no. They don't even know I gamble. Please, Mr. Mancini. They're innocent in all of this. They think I got a job and I'm living just fine at the docks." Ah, nothing worse than being deceived by your only child.

"Shame. After everything they've done for you, you let them down like this." The deeper I press my knife, the higher Kevin's screams get. "Who gave you the fucking envelope?"

Then, there it is. The pop of one of his testicles. Blood stains his cargo shorts in less than five seconds as he screams into the emptiness of the warehouse, spit and blood flying from his mouth.

"Kevin, this is the part where you tell me who gave you the fucking envelope." I'm already bored with this guy. "Look, I'm certain your parents have no fucking clue what a loser you are, so it'd be a shame to have to end them. Do the right thing, Kevin. Save their lives."

On cue, Enzo brings up his phone and there, on the screen, is Kevin's clueless mother serving apple pie to one of my men playing the part of a missionary collecting money for the homeless children. "Talk, asshole. All I have to do is give the signal and your mother is worm food." I look over at Enzo and raise a brow. Harsh? Yes. But also true.

"It don't matter. If I talk, they'll kill them too." Fucking finally. Now we're getting somewhere.

"Give me a fucking name, Kevin. I'll kill your whole goddamn family if I have to. I want the fucking name."

On a sob and with my guy thanking Mrs. Moss for her delicious apple pie, asking if that's cinnamon that she added to the recipe, Kevin finally gives me what I already knew.

"Ugo Ambrosio."

*Bingo.*

Walking around Kevin, I pull his head back and whisper in his ear.

"You did good. Your parents have our protection for your good deed but you, Kevin, scared my wife, and for that, there's nothing on this planet that can protect you from me. Any last wishes?"

"I'm sorr—" He doesn't have time to finish his apology before my knife slices through his vocal chords from one side of his neck clear through to the other, taking his life right along with it.

Nobody fucks with my wife.

"Yeah."

Glancing up at Enzo as he answers his phone, I wipe my knife clean and groan when I see the blood splatter all over my shirt. Good thing I always bring a change of clothes for these events.

"For fuck sake."

That gets my attention.

"When?"

Jesus, I do not like his tone.

"We're on our way."

"Who was that?" Three of our guys arrive and start cleaning up. I nod at them, not knowing their names, but sure I've seen one of them around before.

"Justin said River sneaked out. He can't find her." His words don't compute because if they did, it would sound a lot like River's missing and my brain cannot fucking handle one more goddamn fire.

"Where the fuck is she?" My voice is anything but calm, even though an outsider would never guess. It's the fire burning each of my syllables that gives my rage away.

"No clue. Lina says she didn't notice River's absence." Enzo's about as convinced by my little sister as I am.

"Bullshit." The word pushes out through gritted teeth.

"Agreed."

I quickly try to go over the different places she would have gone. Her brother's, but that seems counterproductive since we're trying to keep them safe. Why bring herself to them and put them in harm's way?

"Rapture?" That was my second guess, but Enzo beat me to it. We'd argued about it just as I was leaving, but I never thought she'd be reckless enough to leave the property.

"Yeah, let's go."

Two hours later, still no River. We missed her at Rapture by about thirty minutes according to her secretary. Something about one of her girls being sexually assaulted by a john. The safety of her employees is at the top of River's list on any given day. She knows what it's like to be put in a perilous situation without a support team to back them up.

So, of fucking course, she put herself in harm's way to come to the aid of her girls. I don't need to tell Enzo that I want someone to beat the fuck out of whoever it is that forced my wife to put herself in danger. We won't kill him, but he won't be able to get his rocks off again. Ever.

By the time we arrive at my mother's house, I am fucking livid and my palms are itching for a punishment.

Except, when I slam the door open and call out for my wife, I get fucking crickets.

"Where the fuck is she?"

Lina is practically yawning at my caveman antics and the fact that I can make grown men piss their fucking pants when I'm calm but, here, I am losing my fucking shit and my sister looks bored out of her mind, doesn't escape me.

"She's fine. Get a hold of yourself."

Enzo growls behind me like he's annoyed at her nonchalance as much as I am.

"Looking for me?"

My head whips around at the sound of River's voice and instead of feeling relief at seeing her safe and sound, my lip curls and my eyes zero in on her mouth, now hanging open. Why the fuck is she in shock? Following her gaze, I realize she's looking at my shirt. The one I didn't have time to change because her little escapades distracted me enough to forget I was wearing blood all over my clothes.

"What did you do?" Her words are whispered but she can't distract me anymore.

"Upstairs. Now."

"What happened?"

Holy fucking shit, if she doesn't run her ass up those goddamn stairs right fucking now, I'm going to spank that beautiful ass in front of every fucking body. Including my mother.

"River, I swear to fucking God, get your ass upstairs, now." My hands are fisted, my nostrils flaring with the last remaining ounce of patience I have left.

"But…"

Fuck this.

In mere seconds, I'm on her, my shoulder in her stomach as I pull her up and over in a fireman's hold. I don't pass Go. I don't collect jack all. I just make a beeline for our bedroom, where I plan to teach my disobedient wife that putting herself in danger is a line I won't tolerate her fucking crossing.

Within the privacy of our quarters, I slide River down my body and strip every last stitch of her clothes right off until she's naked in front of me.

"Are you hurt?"

Any other time, her concern would warm my heart, but right now, the only thing I want warm is the flesh of her ass cheeks as I paint them red.

"No. Get on the fucking bed." She's a little too eager as she jumps on the mattress and sprawls herself out like a present. Christ, this woman is going to be the end of me.

"No, Tesoro. On all fours. Give me your ass." She frowns and I realize she's probably thinking back to when I fucked her hard then left. That was a lesser me. A me who didn't realize that losing her meant losing myself. "Remember what I said about you getting punished for being reckless?"

"Marco, I had to go. One of my girls—" I slice my hand through the air in the universal sign for quit talking.

"I know. I went to Rapture, got the whole story from Taylor." Pulling my shirt off, I throw it in the trash of the en-suite bathroom. "Doesn't mean I'm okay with you sneaking out like a fucking rebellious teenager. What the fuck, River?"

"Kelsey needed my help. Well, she needed my support and I owe it to those girls to be there for them." I love this woman and I love how fierce she is with those around her, but fuck my life... I can't lose her.

"I don't fucking care if Mary Magdelene in person begs you for your help. What part of lock down did you not comprehend?" My breaths are erratic, my heart rate so high I fear my chest will explode from the stress of it all.

"Who is Mary Magdalene?"

For fuck sake. That's what her brain snags on?

"She's... never mind. Get on all fours." Finally, she listens to me. And not a minute too soon.

Kneeling behind her, I bring my head to her ass cheek and lick a path from her thigh to the middle of her ass then, without holding myself back, I bite her. Hard. I leave a mark for her to remember me and my worry every time she decides to sit down.

I expect her to cry out in pain or turn around and call me all the colorful names in her arsenal but instead, my little vixen moans.

She fucking moans like I've just licked her pussy clean.

No woman has ever been more perfect for me than my wife, but I have to remember I'm not very happy with her decision-making skills.

With her ass high in the air and her chest resting against the mattress, I push her down with one hand while the other rains down on her other ass cheek.

"What did I ask you to do, Tesoro?" Rubbing the newly pink flesh with tenderness, I slide my hand down between her legs and smile at her wetness. She's liking this a little too much for it to be a punishment, but fuck it.

Discarding the rest of my clothes, I make my way to the bedside table and open the drawer where I've stashed a bottle of lube. She doesn't miss a beat and before I'm even kneeling behind her, she spreads her thigh even wider, giving me all access, just the way I like it.

"Look at me when you answer me." River's head is turned to the side, her gaze on me, and only me. Holding the bottle of lube up high, I part her cheeks with one hand while the other squeezes the lube until a steady stream is dripping over her crack. She jumps at first contact, the temperature surely a bit colder than her flaming flesh, but she'll survive.

"You told me to stay home."

I use a finger to spread the gel around her puckered hole.

"And what did you choose to do?" One finger slides easily inside, breaching her ring of muscles while my cock slides into her pussy. We both moan at the perfection that is us.

"I went to The City."

I pull out then slam right back in while my finger stays lodged inside her, making her impossibly tighter.

"Did it occur to you that I would be worried?" I push in a second finger, scissoring and preparing her hole for my cock.

"Yes. But—"

"No buts."

Well, except for this one that I'm about to fuck into next week.

"Yes."

Well, at least she thought of me. But still, she went. I continue fucking her pussy nice and slow, taking my time, making her wait for it. I don't want to hurt her, I just need her to understand that her safety is my only priority and apparently, she only listens when my dick is talking.

"For a brief moment, I thought you were gone." It's all I need to say, she understands the rest. She understands that my entire life flashed before my eyes because she *is* my entire fucking life.

"I'm sorry, Marco." She's not, but that's okay. As much as I love pretending she submits to me, I love her loyalty and fierce heart even more. Given the chance, she'd do the exact same fucking thing. Except, next time, I'll make sure she has security with her instead of leaving alone.

"Don't be sorry, Tesoro. Be safe." We're both panting as I bring us closer and closer to orgasm, but not yet. Not fucking yet.

Pulling out, I add more lube to my cock and her hole and just as I take my fingers out, I slowly push my entire length into her.

We groan in unison, accepting the beauty of this moment. Her hands are fisting the sheets, her eyes closed with a serene look blessing her gorgeous face. She's completely open to me. Her mind, her soul, her pussy, and her ass.

Slowly, deliberately, I thrust in and out in long, languorous strides while I lean down and cover her upper body with my chest.

My mouth is at her ear as I hold myself steady on one arm and snake my other around her waist to her clit.

"The next time you disobey my orders…" I can practically hear her eye roll and it only turns me on more. "Take your security detail with you."

In a slow, smooth rhythm, I drive in and out of her hole, playing with her clit and rubbing my entire pelvis on her heated ass cheeks every time I bottom out.

"Promise me, you will never." I thrust in. "Leave." I pull out, agonizingly slow. "Alone." I drive right back inside her hot ass. "Again." I recede quickly before plunging back inside her and grinding against her sore ass as my dick tries to get as deep as fucking possible.

My fingers pinch her clit before flicking it again and again, driving her to insanity because she knows that if she comes before I tell her to, it'll all be for nothing.

"That's my good girl." I pull right out of her and turn her around until she's sprawled out on her back with her legs shaking from the need to come.

Her tits are bouncing as I grip her by the ass cheeks and bring her pussy up to my lips without touching her.

"Now, seal your promise with your cum all over my fucking tongue."

The roar that comes from her is wild and unabashed as my finger rubs intense circles around her clit, and my mouth eats her pussy like I'm starved and she's the only meal on the menu.

She comes and I swallow, I lick, and I search out for more. She can barely breathe as I lap her up for every drop she has to give me. When her body finally gives out, I align her ass back up with my dick and push right back inside her.

I fuck her steadily, in and out, until my own orgasm starts a tingle at the base of my spine.

I fuck her hard until I feel her squeezing my cock with her need for me.

Then I look her straight in the eyes and give her the most important part of me as my orgasm takes me over the fucking edge.

"*Ti amo, Tesoro.*"

I come inside her ass with a roar that I swear shakes the foundation of the entire house.

When I'm done, River scrambles up and wraps her arms around my neck, her mouth on mine as she tastes herself on my tongue. My hands fist her hair, my teeth mark her lips, her neck, her tits, before I go back and devour her mouth all over again.

"I promise."

That's all I need to feel better.

I spend the next hour caring for my wife. A warm towel to clean her up and a hot bath to relax her muscles, I even remember to add the bath salts Lina suggested I buy in bulk. I'll have to make sure I thank her for that. Mostly, as we lie together in the comfort of the hot water, I feel whole with River safe in my arms.

# Chapter Thirteen

## River

I t's been nearly four weeks since the last red envelope, two weeks since Marco showed up covered in blood, and one week since we returned from the Hamptons—on my insistence. I understand Marco's need to keep us all safe, and that's easier when we're all in one place, but being away from my new businesses is detrimental to my employees.

He left a security detail in the Hamptons with his mom, Lina, and Bruce—man, I miss that cute little fluffball. I have my own security detail too, although it's not as bad as I'd imagined. Justin and Aly are like ghosts, stealthier than Enzo or Stefano have ever been, and I forget they're around half the time.

Today, I think they're about to experience something new, and I can't help smirking to myself when I imagine not just them, but Marco as well, camping with my family and me. It's the Summer Equinox, something we've always celebrated with a camping trip, and we do enjoy our little traditions.

The morning sun is shining bright through the open window of the bedroom as I contort my body into an amazing stretch before rolling out of bed.

"Signora Mancini, are you awake?" Stefano's voice is followed by a gentle knocking at the door.

"I am, come in, Stefano." I quickly wrap my fluffy red robe around my otherwise naked body—I don't want him to die after accidentally seeing me naked.

He enters with all the grace of a thousand swans, a tray of pastries and coffee in one hand and a rolling travel suitcase in the other. I raise a brow at the case, curious as to why it's here. Stefano must notice my confusion, clearing his throat as he places the tray down on my bedside table.

"Il Signor Mancini said you would be needing this for your camping trip today."

The burst of laughter that escapes me is impossible to hold in, but I immediately feel bad because Stefano's face is a picture of the confusion I felt moments ago.

"Sorry. Thank you, Stefano. I appreciate it, but I am already packed up. My rucksack is all I need." I nod my head over to my new black bag sitting by the closet door.

Fresh underwear, a sleeping bag, blanket, toiletries, snacks, and a few bottles of water are all I need.

He furrows his brows, seemingly still confused. "But... you are staying away tonight, si? Camping?"

"Yup. Under the stars, *au natural*." I wag my eyebrows, delighting in the fact that his mouth parts and his eyes widen all at the same time, but only for a split second, because a huge grin spreads across his face when he realizes I'm joking about the au natural part.

He slowly shakes his head in amusement as he turns and leaves the room, taking the suitcase with him. Never one for too many words, Stefano only says what is necessary.

Once I'm showered and dressed in yoga pants and a comfy red off-the-shoulder top, I bound down the stairs with my rucksack. I'm surprised to find Marco already waiting for me, a wide smile on his face and too many bags for one person to carry sitting by the front door.

"Erm, you do know we're only camping for one night, don't you?" Placing my rucksack down, I snake my arms around Marco's waist and stare into those beautiful steel-gray eyes.

"*Si.* Is this too much?" The genuine confusion on his face makes me want to ravage him right here and now. It's not very often this big mafia boss man is in new territory, but it seems he's about to land straight into it. His willingness to join me and my family in all things is something I never thought I'd get outside of Kai, but I do, and so much more.

"Baby, you're always too much, but we make it work." With a searing kiss, followed by a sultry wink, I spin on my heel, pick up my rucksack, and head to the front door. "Let's go, Husband."

"Baby *and* Husband. I could get used to the cute names. Although, I'm a little jealous that Everest gets something manly, like Bear." He prowls toward me, grabbing my throat and pushing me to back up against the wall before planting his lips on mine. The urge to grind against him is strong, but we have plans with my family and I don't want to be late.

I manage to pull away from him with a nip on his lower lip, smirking up at him as he raises a brow.

"Don't get used to the cute names though, you're still an asshole." He loosens his grip and I duck under his strong arms in the direction of the door again. "Come on. Which Earth killer are we using today, Monster?"

The guys are off gathering wood for the campfire while Petal, Freya, and I relax in the ideal spot for one of the best views of Manhattan. It's truly glorious with the sun setting; the light hitting buildings and casting shadows makes for a picturesque image. The Hudson practically glitters around the Statue of Liberty, and a wave of calm washes over me.

"How's married life treating you then, Riv?" I'm surprised Freya is beginning a conversation with me. She's been pretty quiet up to this point, and I've kind of left her to it.

"It's great, like nothing I've ever experienced before, and we're really happy." I don't know why I felt the need to tell her we're really happy, I have nothing to prove, but I'm trying to be nice, I suppose. Engage in conversation with her like a grown-ass adult rather than hissing in her annoying face. "How are *you* doing?" Kai mentioned alternative treatments a few weeks ago, and she still doesn't look quite right, so I have an inkling as to how she's doing, but again, nice and polite.

"The doc thinks the new treatment is working, I should be raring to go again in a couple of months." She doesn't look in my direction as she speaks, just continues to look out at the beautiful skyline.

Petal is on her camp chair between us with her eyes closed, shoes and socks off so her bare feet can connect with the earth, and I know she's listening to every word. I also know that what Freya is saying doesn't sound completely true. Research is one of my things, I've always enjoyed it, so of course, I researched Freya's condition and treatment options. The twelve-week course? True. What's happening now? I'm not so sure. Unless she has liver failure, but I somehow doubt that.

"Oh, that's good then. Glad it's all going well." I can only be polite to this woman for so long, and we've got all night to go yet. Whatever she's hiding, I'm going to get to the bottom of it. I have a feeling she's taking Kai for a ride.

"It means I can be your doula now that I'm well enough. I'm so excited to begin preparing."

That gets Petal moving. Her eyes pop open and it looks like she's taking a few subtle deep breaths before responding to that one. My reaction isn't much better. If I had anything in my mouth, it would have made a quick exit.

"We've already found one, actually. A lovely lady named Lydia. Brad and Ginny recommended her, so we met up a few times and she's perfect. Sorry Frey." She speaks so calmly, injecting her usual sunshine into her words to help make light of the disappointing news she's breaking. Petal excitedly told me all about Lydia a couple of weeks ago and I'm already looking forward to meeting her.

Freya visibly deflates and we sit in peaceful silence for a little while longer as the sun continues to get lower in the sky. I would have simply told her to go fuck herself, but this is where Petal and I differ. She and Ev are the light to my dark, the joy to my pain, and I'm damn proud of them both.

"You ladies finished gazing into space and ready to come jump over some fire?"

Heavy hands grip my shoulders, beginning to slowly massage at my muscles. It feels divine. I tip my head back to look up at Marco grinning above me. His stubbled face is as picturesque as the view in front of us and I smile right back at him, amazed at how he can make my clit tingle with just one look.

"We are."

He leans down, gripping my chin to tilt my head back further to meet his mouth, and devours me in the sexiest Spiderman kiss in existence.

"Dude, that's my sister."

Marco pulls away from me with a smirk and I laugh at my brother's disgust.

"Kai, can you carry my chair for me please? It might be a little too much for me to take it myself."

Freya's whiney voice grates on my nerves as I pack away my own chair, sliding it into the convenient carry-case and throwing it over my shoulder. Petal doesn't even get a choice as Everest does the same with her chair. And as Marco goes to take mine from me, I glare at him, raising a questioning brow, letting him know I'm a big girl who doesn't need my man to carry my shit. Being pregnant would be the only time I'd allow it, and I don't plan on doing that anytime soon.

Shaking his head in amusement, Marco interlocks his fingers with mine and we all head toward our camping spot.

By the time we make it back, the sun has almost fully set and the moon is just visible in the sky. There's a chill in the air with the light wind, but it's bearable and we have plenty of blankets at the ready. I allow Marco to set up my camping chair next to his while I start the fire. It's not too big for now; we have some jumping to do before we use it for heat.

"Who's first this year?" I look around the group, smiling at Marco's confusion. I haven't told him about this part yet.

"Ooh, me!"

Of course it's fucking Freya. I stand, gesturing for her to come closer. Petal stands as well, encouraging the others to do the same and grabbing Ev and Marco by the hand. I reach out for Marco's other hand, and Kai, who's on the other side of me.

"I know you're new to all of this, Marco, but I just want to say thank you for allowing us to embrace you into our world. We know it's not for everyone, and we know this year has been tough. So here's to new beginnings. Are we all ready?"

"Duh, I've been ready for ages."

This is why we didn't invite Freya to this last year, she's a total attention hog. As soon as someone else is getting any kind of praise, she's there, ready to shit all over it.

Petal rolls her eyes and takes a deep breath, closing her eyes and tilting her head to the sky. "Let the energy of the Summer Solstice help you release, recharge, and bring you balance."

Ev, Kai, and I repeat her words, with Marco joining in halfway through when he realizes what we're doing.

We all watch as Freya jumps over the small fire, then we cheer to her new beginnings. Maybe she'll be less of a bitch this year...

She heads straight for Kai when she's finished, with an angry glance at where our hands are joined, immediately interjecting herself in his place. "Why don't you go next, Kai?"

He shrugs and moves to stand in front of the fire. We repeat the process for him, Ev, then me, and I'm not entirely sure if Marco's going to do it or not, but he eagerly steps forward. He comes straight for me when he's finished his jump over the fire, wrapping me in his arms and lifting me, spinning me in a circle and kissing my neck.

"This is fun. Thank you for including me, Tesoro."

I could get used to this carefree side of him. I know Aly and Justin are around somewhere being all stealthy and shit, plus a few others whose names I don't know, and there are still some dangerous things going on, but tonight is special for so many reasons.

Petal steps forward, ready for her jump, and I see the moment Ev decides that's not happening. But he calls Kai over and they both stand either side of her, flanking her.

"What are yo—" Ev nods once at Kai and they both bend, grabbing a thigh each and securing her back, lifting her over and across the fire as she squeals in delight before they place her gently down again.

Her giggle brings back all the sunshine and I know this is going to be a great year. How could it not be?

# CHAPTER FOURTEEN

## MARCO

One night away with my favorite little witches so Mother Nature could recharge their earthly bodies—their words and sure as fuck not mine—was all I could spare. Tomorrow night is the pre-opening of the new and improved Mancini Hotel-SoHo. It's our headquarters, the pillar of our chain, and if it doesn't look perfect, it reflects on every site we own.

I must say, I actually do feel somewhat reinvigorated. Doesn't mean the urge to bitch slap Kai didn't come over me once or ten times, but here's the thing: having River as a wife puts a lot of shit into perspective. The value she puts on friendship is something I admire, so for that reason alone, I call upon every ounce of self-control whenever that dude decides to put his hands on my wife.

It's always seemingly innocent. Ruffling her hair, saving her from the imaginary mosquito on her shoulder, thumbing a drop of beer from her bottom lip. Okay, fine. I almost broke his wrist when I intercepted that smooth move.

Little fucker has his own wife. Maybe he should worry about what's coming out of her mouth a little more and a little less about River.

"Heard you went out and got rejuvenated by Mother Nature last night." Tyler stands at the bottom of my stairwell as I trot down, swinging my jacket around and closing the middle button. "You still look like an old bastard to me. Guess it didn't work, huh?"

As I reach the last step, I walk right up to his smug face and slap his cheek like I'm the Godfather and he's my minion. "Don't be jealous, Tyler. Not a good look on you, brother."

Chuckling, he shakes his head and follows me out where Enzo is waiting for us. Tonight, we're taking the limo so we can enjoy ourselves at the club. With everything ready for tomorrow, I don't need to be at the hotel until late in the morning to sign off on the last-minute changes that are inevitable for the kind of party we've planned.

Before all that, we're going to surprise my wife at her workplace, so I can watch her in her element and support her in her endeavors. Also, who the fuck doesn't enjoy a good burlesque show?

"Madelina texted me earlier saying she had a few clients staying late at the salon. I figured if I told her where we were going, she'd out us to River." Tyler's fingers are flying across the screen of his phone as he types whatever it is he's saying to my sister. With my back to the driver, I have Enzo and Tyler sitting side by side and, like this, they couldn't look any more different. Tyler is the epitome of the billionaire mogul with his effortless good looks, broody charisma, and eyes so dark, grown men cower across the conference room when it's time to make a deal.

Enzo, on the other hand, is rough around the edges with more bulk than finesse. His past weighs heavily on his shoulders which, like Tyler, has men begging for mercy before he's even begun to torture them.

Yet, these two knuckleheads are like well-trained pups when it comes to Lina. At least, that's how it looks on my end.

That said, Enzo thinks I've handed my balls to River for her to do with as she wishes, but what he doesn't realize is that she knows exactly how to roll them around her palm and make me come straight down her throat. So, if that makes me pussy whipped, then so fucking be it.

"What are you looking at, asshole?" My gaze slides to Tyler and my grin widens. A hundred bucks says Lina's answer was not what he was expecting or wishing.

My father always said, "The bigger you are, the harder you'll fall."

Well, *boom*, mother fuckers, we've come crashing down.

We have time for a couple of Old Fashioneds before we reach Rapture. As always, New York City traffic is a bitch and there's nothing to be done about it except sit back, relax, and enjoy these rare moments with childhood friends.

Tyler, Nate, and I were fast friends because our circumstances and our family-ties naturally brought us together. We were inseparable throughout the years in school and when we went to our preferred colleges, we still kept in touch like we were legit brothers.

Enzo, on the other hand, was like an adopted brother my father saved from the streets. It was difficult to be openly friends outside the house. We were both teenagers, but where I had a life of privilege, Enzo was already learning the trade of torture and surviving as a mob soldier.

Nate's death has left a small hole in my black heart, especially when my mind wanders down memory lane, but

I've grieved his betrayal and I hope he's in a better place, with Angelica at his side. I truly hope he's happy.

As we pull up to the club, Tyler whistles when he sees the line hugging straight down the wall and around the corner. My wife has turned this place into one of The City's hottest night spots. Fuck, she makes me proud.

"I knew she was smart, but I didn't realize just how savvy our girl, River is."

Glaring at Tyler, I point my index finger at him and snarl, "She's not *our* girl, fucker. She's *my* wife." Fuck, I love Tyler but every time he says something that reminds me that he had her before me, it drives me to the edge of my sanity.

"Sorry, man." He shrugs and has the decency to look sheepish. "I just meant, she deserves this, you know?"

I grunt like the caveman I've apparently turned into before punching his shoulder.

"Come on, let's surprise the owner."

As we reach the entrance, the host smiles and lets us in with a "Go on in, sir," as she unhooks the red corded rope and secures it back once we've cleared inside.

Just as we walk in, the mood is set. Black and red furniture with strategically placed poles on round stages line the sides of both walls. The women on this floor aren't naked, but their costumes are so intricate and sexy that it feels even more intimate. Every single velvet couch and deep-seated chair is taken; the place is full to the brim.

I've been here before, during the day, as the performers practice and the servers take inventory, but I've never actually seen it at its prime.

If I was impressed before, I'm fucking flabbergasted at the sight of River's hard work and impeccable vision.

"Holy shit, this place is going to be a gold mine." Tyler's impressed and it just makes me even prouder of River.

I scan the floor, hoping to see the most stunning woman in existence, and spot her with ease. Standing tall with her shoulders squared and her chin up, she's talking to a couple of businessmen who find whatever she's saying to be fascinating.

She's not flirting or putting her sexuality up for grabs, she's talking shop and they're loving every single moment of it. *Sorry, assholes, she's coming home with me tonight. And every night after.*

Just to the right of where she's standing, I see an empty table with a two-seater couch and an armchair. It's perfect for us, center stage and easy access for the servers.

The fact that it forces me to walk past my wife is just an added bonus.

I wait until I'm just behind her, my chest pressing to her back before I grin up at the two businessmen and whisper in River's ear. "You look absolutely mouth-watering right now. What are the chances I can whisk you away to feast on you?" Without missing a beat, River angles herself just enough to introduce me to the men.

"Mr. Bordas, Mr. Shoemaker, this is my husband, Marco Mancini. Marco, these two gentlemen are here from the mayor's office." Well damn, word is obviously getting out.

"Gentlemen, a pleasure." We shake hands as my left arm wraps around River's waist, bringing her closer to me.

"Please excuse us and enjoy your evening." River, ever the professional, changes completely as she whips around and loses a little of her perfect veneer.

"What the fuck are you doing here?" I frown, my eyes searching her features as her gaze travels around the club like she's scanning for someone.

"Tesoro, I don't know whether to punish that delicious mouth of yours with a heavy dose of my cock or drape you over my knee and show your clientele what happens to your ass when you misbehave." Her gaze returns to me, but she's quickly distracted by something over my shoulder.

"Enzo and Tyler are here?" Did she just squeak? What the fuck is happening right now?

As if the lights weren't dim enough, the room sinks into complete darkness as a spotlight illuminates the stage in reds and purples and deep blues.

"Please don't be mad." I frown at River's words, but let her lead me to the table where Tyler and Enzo are pouring three glasses of scotch and sitting back, ready to enjoy the show.

I don't have time to ask River why she's being so sketchy when the first notes of a sultry ballad entrance the entire room. My wife kisses me hard on my lips, palming both my cheeks and looking me straight in the eyes. "Just remember, keep an open and forgiving mind." Then she's gone, leaving me to wonder what the actual fuck is going on.

Sitting on one end of the couch, I grab my glass of scotch as the silhouette of a young woman on center stage grabs everyone's attention. Her heels are impossibly high, sparkling with every reflection from the spotlight. They match perfectly with her barely-there sequin dress, partially hidden by a long curtain of dark hair reaching the small of her back.

Bringing one leg straight up to the pole and wrapping it around until she's upside down, I notice the three of us are angling our heads to the side like it'll help us understand how this woman is able to contort her body in this way.

"What the actual fuck?" Tyler growls to my left while Enzo mumbles a not so discreet, "Shit." It takes me a few seconds longer to understand their reactions.

In fact, I only clue in once the woman spins around to the beat of the music with her head upside down and faces us, her legs straight up and in a vee as she holds the bar effortlessly. That's when it dawns on me, and River's words finally make sense.

"Jesus fucking Christ, is that my baby sister?"

# Chapter Fifteen

## River

"How mad is Marco about last night?" Lina checks her reflection in the mirror as she applies the final touches of her cherry-red lipstick. She's a vision in midnight-blue this evening, with crystals glittering on the bust of her sweetheart neckline every time they catch the light. As is usual for Lina, her formal attire consists of a figure-hugging floor-length gown with an almost indecent split to show off her left leg. Her long, dark hair is pinned up in a mass of glorious curls, with loose tendrils falling all around, exactly how they were designed to.

"Do you really wanna know what my punishment was for keeping that secret from your brother?" Turning from the vanity, I give her my best innocent and questioning face.

"Ew, no!"

Laughing, I finish sweeping mascara across my lashes and take one final look at my reflection. The longer side of my hair is styled into my face in messy waves, the short-er side with some volume but gripped back, emphasizing the beautiful crystal moon drop earrings Marco surprised me with this morning. He actually found the whole Lina working at my club thing amusing, and a few light spanks followed by a couple of mind-blowing orgasms was all the 'punishment' I received, but it's fun to make Lina think otherwise.

"You've got nothing to worry about with your big brother, but you do owe me! The real question here should be, how mad are Tyler and Enzo about last night?"

Standing, I move to sit on Lina's bed, where she has all our shoe options laid out across the blankets. I choose a simple red pair of Jimmy Choos, covered in silver glitter—okay, maybe not so simple, but they're super pretty. They go perfectly with the red knee-length pen-cil-skirt-style dress I'm wearing, and when I attach the long and floaty sparkly skirt section—like a cape but for the waist, it's my new favorite dress—they'll go even better still.

"Well, I think Enzo already knew, but I can't be sure. He was his usual broody self, a few grunts here and there—and not the sexual kind." She giggles at her own joke, and I join her. Her excitable and fun aura is infectious, and this is one reason I was never able to cut this woman out of my life. "Tyler, on the other hand, gave me the fifth degree about being safe, showing off my body to dirty old men with bad thoughts, keeping secrets... ya know, all the things, because it's Tyler and when he loses control it sends him spiraling."

"Yeah, I know. At least the truth's out now though. No more sneaking around or trying to lose your security team... although, if Enzo knew, I doubt that you were losing them half as much as you think. You know he's a freaking ninja when it comes to all things safety."

"I do. And I also know how ridiculous it was to believe I was duping him or his team all this time, but fuck it. What's done is done, and I'm ready to enjoy my big brother's fancy pre-launch party thing."

Lina is much like me, in that we can compartmentalize whatever shit may be going on to be there for family when they need us. And tonight, Marco needs us. As much as he hides it from the rest of the world, my husband is nervous about this pre-opening launch of his hotel. It's the first time he hasn't had his father's help with something of this magnitude, and I can see how much that fact hurts him.

We are the first people to arrive, and my gods, this place is glorious. The hotel is very similar to before, but it's been updated and elevated to a level I never imagined possible. It's like stepping into Italy itself, and modern luxury has all been intertwined with historic lines, it honestly couldn't be more perfect.

"No, you didn't!" There are servers lining one of the walls, with various appetizers on their gold-plated trays ready for when the guests begin arriving any moment, and as I'm grabbing myself a glass of something bubbly from one of them, I can't contain my joy at what I'm seeing.

"I did, Tesoro. I couldn't do this evening without a little something my wife would approve of."

There, mixed in with other chocolates on the tray, are teeny chocolate penises. Just like the ones I made Stefano use for the Christmas Eve party. It almost brings a tear to my eye, but I suck that fucker right back inside.

"You're a slick motherfucker, aren't you? You were getting some tonight already, but this…? Well, I'm going to have to come up with an extra surprise for you too now." I wink at my husband as I stroke a hand across his shirt-covered chest.

"You could just give me your panties."

"Who says I'm wearing any?"

"Fuck." The word is said on such a deep growl that it sends shivers down my spine, and as I tense up, the love eggs—part of my punishment for keeping the Lina-secret from Marco—send a whole other shiver through me. Marco grips the back of my head and pulls my lips to meet his, his other hand grasping at my hip, no doubt leaving delicious bruises as a reminder of his ownership. Much like the crescent-shaped marks I left on his back last night after gripping him so hard I broke a pinky nail.

"Mmm. Mine." He breathes the words over my parted lips and I smile up at him as I reach my hands around to squeeze his delectable ass before tapping it lightly.

"Come on, Mr. Mancini, time to play host."

As guests begin to arrive, filling in the open space in the grand hall just off the main lobby, I play the dutiful wife. Making polite conversation, gushing about the renovations, none of it feels like it used to when I literally 'played the part', it's different somehow. I actually mean the words that are coming out of my mouth—well, the ones about my husband anyway.

A string orchestra is in the far corner of the room, looming glass windows behind them as they play. The lyrical sounds of modern classics fill the space, creating an amazing atmosphere of class and elegance. When they begin playing *Demons*, the first song Marco and I danced to, a grin spreads across my face and I tug at his arm.

To hear it being played in this way, no words, is beautiful, and Marco looks down at me with pure love in his stormy eyes.

"Please excuse me, I must dance with my wife." He's speaking to the important men in front of us, but his gaze is solely on me and he doesn't wait for a response from them before he turns to me, sliding his hands around my waist.

We don't move to the area set up for dancing, no one is there anyway, instead, he focuses all his attention on me as we begin to sway to the music floating through the room. My arms are around his neck and I can't help tickling my fingers over his skin, tangling them in the short strands of his hair.

Our bodies move seamlessly together and the rest of the world seems inconsequential in this moment. All that exists are the two of us as I rest my head against Marco's chest, breathing in the vanilla scent that calms everything inside me, that makes me strong.

Before the song is finished, Marco stiffens in my hold, muttering something unintelligible as he gently pulls away.

"Marco, sweetie. How lovely to see you."

An older woman with silver hair approaches, dripping in jewels and sequins, and she offers him her hand as if she's royalty.

"Eleonor, I didn't know you were coming this evening. How are you?" Marco, ever the gentleman, politely holds her hand, tipping his head before letting go.

"Oh, Marco. I'm still a complete mess. Elizabeth persuaded me to come with her. Just to get out of the house, you know? Have you heard anything yet?"

This woman has to be Elizabeth's mother or a friend. Either way, I don't like the vibes she's giving off, so I allow my trusty mask to slip into place as I smile sweetly at her—even though she seems to be completely ignoring my presence. Marco squeezes my hand gently, as if he can sense my unease with this woman.

"No news at the moment, I'm afraid. Like I said, I doubt he'd want to speak with me anyway after our last encounter."

*Who is he talking about?*

"Yes, yes, you did say. But you know people. Influential people. If anyone can find my boy, my Nathaniel, it's you." The woman dabs at invisible tears at the same time that my insides all decide to shoot up my throat, fear gripping me at the mention of Nathaniel's name.

This woman is Nathaniel's mother. *Oh, fuck.*

"I will continue to do my best, Ms. Hunter."

"I know you will. You've always been a sweet boy. I must go to the ladies' room and tidy myself up a little. I'm such a mess. Thank you, Marco."

She swiftly turns, fake tears and all, continuing to pretend I don't exist, and disappears into the crowd of people. While all this is happening, my body is shutting down and I'm finding it hard to breathe properly. Marco must sense something is wrong, as he wraps an arm around me, leads me from the room, up a flight of stairs and out onto a balcony. He remains stoically silent until we reach our destination, then crumbles right along with me as my legs finally give out.

He holds me tightly, stroking a hand up and down my back as I nestle into him, allowing him to be strong for me in this moment while I freak the fuck out. The mention of Nathaniel's name brought the vision of him lying in the hall of my old apartment into the forefront of my mind, and it's difficult to shake. His pale skin, the blood...

Nope. I'm not doing this.

I take a deep breath, becoming aware of the chill in the air as my surroundings come into focus. Deep inhale, deep exhale. And again.

"Okay, I'm good. Thank you." I speak into his chest, enjoying the comfort of his warmth.

"You sure, Tesoro?" He places a gentle kiss on the top of my head.

"Mmmhmm." Another deep breath.

My eyes shoot open then, as I remember I have fucking questions. I wriggle out of his lap, standing and leaning against the banister of the balcony, paying zero attention to the beauty that is SoHo at night. "What the fuck was that all about, Marco? Obviously, that was Nathaniel's mother, and it sounded a lot like this wasn't your first conversation about where he is. So, it's time for you to fess up, Mr. Mancini. I've been patient and understanding, but you've got a fuckload to explain. I fucking love you, Marco, but I'm sick and tired of the secrets and avoidance. It ends tonight."

Lifting my dress and putting my hands in between my legs, I remove the love eggs sitting inside my pussy and throw them at him. He catches them—asshole—silently pulling out a silky red handkerchief from his suit pocket and wrapping them up. His silence is deafening, and I'm aware this is the first time I've used the *L* word with him, but it came out involuntarily. I mean it with every inch of my soul and would never take it back, but if he thinks I'm going to continue to act like a wife, be a wife, what the fuck ever, then he needs to start talking.

He moves toward me, his lustful intentions clear in his steel-gray eyes.

"Te—"

"No. I don't want to hear it right now. I'm tired, I'm angry, and I've just had a pretty big shocker dropped at my feet. Especially after being told it was all dealt with. So, thanks for that. You need to go back inside and be the host. I will stay here until it's time to go home, because I'm not fucking stupid and about to go wandering around at night by myself. Who knows what other lies and secrets you have? The dude leaving notes is probably down-fuck-ing-stairs in that ballroom sipping champagne and eating penis chocolate." When I've finished my rant, I turn and storm toward the door. "I'm going to powder my nose. When I come back, don't be here. I need to be away from you right now, and until you're ready to give me answers, don't speak to me." Then I sashay like a fucking queen all the way to the ladies' room without looking back.

After a few dabs of cold water on my cheeks, because I don't want to walk out of here looking like Alice Cooper, I take in my appearance in the mirror. I look myself dead in the eyes, determination and strength shining through.

"You are a badass bitch. You are not alone anymore, you have a fucking army at your fingertips. Nothing will break you."

I take another much-needed deep breath and smile at my reflection. I just dropped the love bomb on Marco and ran away. Right after finding out the man I killed in self-defense is classed as missing rather than playing doctor around the world, according to his mother. This is all fucked in so many ways, and as much as I need the answers I'm so desperately seeking, I'm not walking away. I trust that Marco has it in hand, but he needs to start trusting me, and the fact that I'm ready and willing to stand by his side in all things in return. I could do without all the blood and shit, but in the name of protecting my family, count me in.

"Hey, River." One of the stall doors opens slowly and Elizabeth shows herself. Great, she's been sitting in there the whole time and likely heard my little speech to myself. "Sorry, I figured you were having a moment, so I kind of left you to it, but it started to feel a bit weird sitting in there all this time and I didn't want you to think I was… well, you know, taking a crap." She smiles and shrugs her shoulders, and I snort-laugh.

Fuck, I needed that.

It seems so out of character to her usual cold and sophisticated self that I almost like her.

"I didn't even realize you were in there, to be honest." I'm in badass bitch, answer-getting mode, so fuck it. "While I have you alone. I think you and I should talk."

She doesn't look shocked by my words, more like she's accepting, knowing we need to do this as much as I do.

"I agree."

The fact that she brought Eleonor, Mrs. Hunter, Nathaniel's mom, whoever the fuck the old lady is, with her this evening is something I'm going to let slide for now. That's a Marco problem.

"Marco is my husband, which I know damn well you're aware of, so I don't know what you think you're doing by continuing to insert yourself into his life as you have been, but it needs to stop. He's never going to be yours and the fact that you haven't realized that yet is a little sad."

I'm aware that I'm coming across as a complete bitch with her, and I feel a little bad about it, but it's nothing she hasn't inflicted on me and she needs to hear what I have to say.

"You are right. I know."

Her admission surprises me. I expected her to fight back a little, but nothing. Complete agreement.

"I am right, yes." I don't know what else to say so I just watch her, dumbfounded, as she casually washes her hands, a small smile on her ruby-red lips.

"I'm bound by my duty to my family, which is something I know you can relate to. After spending time with your friend, Kai, I understand you more now, and I'm sorry. It's just, I don't know how much Marco has told you, but I don't want to be a part of it anymore. Marco has been helping me to find a way out of this. It's not who I want to be. Can we call a truce?"

Well, none of this is what I was expecting, and I still need Marco to fill in all the gaps, but she seems genuine. My people-reading skills don't usually steer me wrong.

"I won't call a truce with someone I never perceived as a threat." Her eyes widen at my admission and she moves to speak before I interrupt her. "But as long as you stop trying to seduce my husband, we can call it quits on all the bitchiness." I'm still going to be prickly about it, but that doesn't mean I can't make it funny at the same time.

"I won't say we're going to suddenly become best friends, because no. But at least we can be civil with each other if you're going to keep popping up everywhere." I laugh and hold out my hand for a formal shake.

She takes it, bringing me closer to air-kiss my cheeks.

"Deal. You're a far better woman than I, River Fox-Mancini."

# Chapter Sixteen

## Marco

I can't remember the last time I was ever afraid of something. Until River, that is. Until that bone-deep fear of losing her took root inside my gut.

Now, every decision I make is centered around her. I just wish I hadn't started off on the wrong foot. I probably should have told her everything from the start, but it's easy to regret when you have hindsight being a judgmental bitch with your conscience.

As promised, River came back from the bathroom last night and waited for me to join her after the party so we could talk.

We left the hotel hand in hand, but our trip was spent with both of us looking out of our respective windows as the driver took us back home. She hasn't spoken to me since.

I've been called a lot of things in my life, but coward was never one of them. Yet, here we are. Here, I am, scared of telling my wife, who finally—fucking finally—told me she loves me. Even if those words were thrown at me like a fucking bazooka instead of being lovingly placed on my lips.

I have everything to lose and if—no, when—I drop my bomb into her lap, it will literally change everything in her life.

Everything she ever thought to be true.

She may never forgive me for this, which is why I need to make sure contingencies are in place in case she decides to finally demand an annulment and walk away for good.

Fuck, the thought has bile rising up my throat.

Opening my eyes and turning my head to the side, I smile at the sight of my beautiful wife sleeping like the dead. She was pissed last night when I didn't show any signs of opening up the valves and letting the truth rush into our lives. At one point, I thought she'd given up the silent treatment as she slowly undressed in front of me and slid between the sheets of our marital bed. When I reached out for her, she placed a soft hand on my cheek and asked, "Are you ready to tell me everything?" When I didn't answer, she just shook her head and turned her back on me.

My punishment was having to sleep next to the most enticing woman in the world and not be allowed to touch her.

Message received, Tesoro. Message received loud and fucking clear.

After this morning's meeting, I'll have all my men in place and she'll be safe, with no more secrets between us. That's when I'll know my fate. That's when I'll know if we'll survive this.

Slipping out of our bed as quietly and softly as humanly possible, I take out a clean suit, socks, and boxer-briefs before heading to the bathroom for a shower.

When I exit the bathroom, a towel resting low on my waist, my gaze naturally goes straight to our bed, expecting to see a sleeping River, all wrapped up in the down comforter. Instead, the bed is empty and my wife is nowhere to be found.

After dressing and taking my gun out from my safe, I brave my way downstairs, where I'm guessing River is praying to the gods of coffee.

I hesitate when I see her curled up with Bruce in the corner of the couch, her glare a living, breathing thing. We stare at each other, unspoken words like an ocean of regret.

I don't know how to fix this right now, so I just nod and as I turn on my heel, she grunts like she wants to rip my balls off and serve them to Bruce for a morning snack.

With Enzo driving and two men from his security team following behind us, we head out to Long Island on a rare day of open roads and little traffic. Thank fuck for Sunday mornings.

"She's there, waiting for us."

I look at my right-hand man, thankful he can practically read my mind.

"Good." I'm accessing the warehouse cameras to make sure there aren't unwanted cars parked nearby or any stragglers hanging around the property. We've kept this place secret for a long time. We store our product here, our guns and our torture room. It's why we bought so much real estate in this area. It keeps the area secluded and empty of prying eyes.

Officially, it's a building we're planning to destroy in order to build something new and shiny in its place. In reality, it's low-key and useful when I don't want to be seen.

"You should have told her from the start. You know that, right?"

*Fuck, not this again.*

"Like you should have told me my sister spends her free time pole dancing for old pervs?" I raise a brow in question, even though his eyes are on the road ahead and can't see the challenge in my features.

"There was nothing to tell. She was safe."

A man of few words, this asshole.

I'm about to tell him he's supposed to be reporting to me with any and all of the shit happening when my phone rings. Stefano's number flashes on my screen and I know for a fact that it has to do with River.

"Mancini."

"*Signore, vostra moglie vuole sapere dove si trova.*" Of course she does. I can't help the smile that creeps up the corners of my lips at the thought that even when she's angry, she still wants to know where I am. Granted, it's because she wants to torture me and maybe even kick my ass up and down the marble floor, but still.

She loves me and I need to hang on to that.

"*Dille che ho un appuntamento.*" Enzo snorts beside me and I shake my head. Fucker. It's not a lie, I do have a meeting, it's just not for business in a classic sense.

"*Bene, Signore. A più tardi.*" I will, indeed, see him later. And River, for that matter. As soon as this meeting is over, she and I will be having a difficult conversation.

Once we arrive in Long Island City, we drive the car into one of the secured garages, close, lock the electric door, and make our way into the side office. As run-down as it looks on the outside, inside, it's comfortable. Far from luxurious, there's no need for that, but it is practical.

A large space for... inciting our guests to divulge information, with an office space to the side that holds a secret bunker-type room in case we need to hide products from any suspicious police officers.

"Boss." J bows her head as we enter the large hall, following Enzo as we make our way to the office. Our security guys are camped outside our doors, checking the cameras the whole time via apps installed on their phones.

"There's been a change of plans." I don't play around, just sit behind the desk and steeple my hands at my lips.

J is immediately on high alert, ready to execute all of my commands. Much like my father did with Enzo, I picked J off the street when she was just seventeen and running drugs to feed her junkie boyfriend. At first, she was a soldier following me around when I was Capo so I could teach her the ropes, give her advice and help her to survive the streets without having to scrounge. Too young to be my sister's security detail, I made sure she was safe under my wing.

Turns out, J has a fascinating mind. She's able to analyze and solve problems with an accuracy I've never seen before. I tried to get her back to school, to cultivate her genius, but she turned me down. The system fucked her over once and she refuses to fall victim to them again.

"I'm declaring a hit on Ugo Ambrosio." J doesn't even flinch. One nod and her eyes glaze over, which means she's calculating and putting a plan in place.

"Timeline?" It's her only question, the rest is up to her and she knows it.

I look to Enzo, who's been working with Stefano on the logistics.

"He won't be in The City for long. We're guessing within the next week, they'll move in and try to either hurt River or take Marco down. Rumor has it, they want a hostile takeover of New York City and they've negotiated with some of the neighboring big shots."

"The Irish?" With their influence in the police force, I figured Ambrosio would start there and J had the same thought.

"No, they've been loyal to us," I answer instead of Enzo. "Let's just say, the Newark police force is getting a hefty donation to keep their streets safe from the mob and gangs." I grin at the irony, but J and Enzo are cut from the same humorless cloth.

"Kastellanos." My lip curls at Enzo's mention of the name I thought my father had buried long ago.

"I've heard rumors, but didn't have any proof of anything happening." J nods as she speaks, almost apologetic.

"Yeah, word on the streets is, Ambrosio traded some land in northern Greece for his support here in taking me down." I almost scoff at the notion that even with the two of them working together, that they'd think they could touch me. "I guess my father underestimated his ambitions."

"So, why not take Giuseppe? Why his son?" J may have spent the last five years here with us, but she still doesn't know all the intricacies of the laws in our world.

"He's a don. It throws off the balance of our system. Going after his son is fair game."

"I mean, he's going after you, isn't he?" I know why she's questioning, she needs to have all the information so she can do her job effectively.

"No, he's going after River. They think she's fair game, but going after River is worse than going after me." The thought makes my veins throb with boiling blood running wild.

"Right. Blind you with anger so you make a mistake. Take away the one thing or person you love most and destroy you from the inside." J repeats my words from years ago.

"Exactly. Except, you're going to take out Ugo, then we'll ship them back to Italy and if they're unwilling… well, I'll personally take out the entire fucking family."

"This information is between us only. We need you to be the executor, not one of your Reapers. We can't take the risk that anyone less qualified than you fuck this job up, *capisci*?" J nods at Enzo just as my phone rings loudly in the near-empty space.

"Mancini."

"Boss, your wife has just pulled up and she's walking up to the front entrance." Fucking Hell. I'm going to kill Stefano for falling for River's charms. Goddammit. "Shit."

"What? What do you mean, shit?" I'm suddenly standing because this guy's worried tone and River's proximity does not reassure me in the least.

"She's being followed by two goons, boss. They seem to—" I cut off the call and run to the front entrance with Enzo and J on my heel. As soon as I get there, the door flies open and my beautiful wife is taken by surprise that I'd be so close.

"We need to—" Grabbing her by the upper arm, I quickly pull her away, practically dragging her to safety. "What the fuck, Marco. Let me go!" I don't answer because all Hell is about to break loose and I cannot have my wife in the middle of a fucking war, except she's fighting me every step of the way as she pulls her arm from my grip and stops in her tracks.

"Will you just stop—" Again, I cut her off by picking her up into a fireman's hold and hauling her off to the bunker. From there, no one will know where she is. She'll be safe while I deal with this shit-show.

Placing her inside, I grab her by the back of the head and look her in the eye as the first shots are fired in the other room.

"I love you, Tesoro, and I need you to stay safe. Promise me."

She's wide-eyed now, probably realizing that danger is knocking on our door. Fuck, I hope I make it back.

"I promise. Don't go, Marco. Don't, please stay—" I kiss her, hard, and breathe my love against her lips.

"I'll be right back." I don't hear the rest of her protests as I close the secured door and run into the mouth of danger.

# Chapter Seventeen

## River

"*Buongiorno*, River." Mrs. Mancini greets me with a warm smile as I enter the dining room, standing to pour me a fresh coffee. This woman gets me.

"Good morning to you too." I sit on the sofa beside her and help myself to a croissant. Bruce notices someone new is in the room and leaps up from his resting spot, bounding over to me on his tiny little legs. I scoop up the bundle of fluff and rest him on my knee as I sip my coffee.

The air in the room changes as Marco enters, looking like sin all wrapped up in a sexy suit, but I won't allow myself to give in to him. He glares at me for longer than is acceptably comfortable, before nodding his head gently and walking away.

*Asshole.*

"Is something wrong with Marco? He didn't say goodbye the way he usually does."

Never one to mince her words, Gabriella Mancini is always straight to the awkward point. I woke up and ambled downstairs, needing coffee for the conversation I was hoping to have this morning. But no, the asshole has clearly decided to go out fuck knows where. Since Gabriella doesn't seem to know where, I'll just have to ask Stefano. Which can wait until I've finished my breakfast because I'm absolutely not rushing to chase after Marco.

"He's in a mood. You know how he can be."

She's not buying it, I can tell by the upturn of one corner of her mouth and the glint in her gray eyes.

"What's going on, *bella*? Talk to me."

The question seems so out of the blue, but also, it feels like an opportunity. Gabriella Mancini has lived in this crazy world, lived as the wife of the don of fucking New York City. She may be a grieving widow, but I still see the fire behind her eyes. Maybe she could help me figure out how to crack the shell that is Marco, spilling all his secrets and finally getting him to let me all the way in. Then I can finally do the same for him.

While he's holding back from me, as much as I've never felt this way before, there's still something holding me back, just a tiny bit.

I sigh, unable to lie, and also strangely unable to keep everything to myself.

"He's keeping things from me." This next part feels childish to say it out loud, but her gaze is full of encouragement instead of the judgment I'm expecting. "So I'm ignoring him until he stops. I'm tired of the secrets."

Gabriella nods her head in understanding. "*Sì.* Good idea. Alberto once tried to keep secrets from me, but he soon realized I was no wilting flower. The day I threatened to burn his beloved car to the ground was when he finally let me all the way in." A wistful look passes through her eyes and she smiles at the memory, laughing softly before fixing me with her gaze once more. "You are a strong Italian woman, River. Just like your grandmother. I know you can get through to that pig-headed son of mine."

Wait, what now?

"Did you know my grandmother? I'm also pretty sure we're not Italian." The only emotion filling me in this moment is confusion. The last time I saw my grandparents was the night my parents died. Then I recall what Gabriella said at the Christmas eve party, something I'd put to the back of my mind. She'd said I look just like *her*. Did she mean my grandmother?

"I did, she was a wonderful woman. Always full of joy. I knew your parents too, before they left the life."

Holy fuck in a bucket, how am I only just hearing all of this information? This feels like something I should know. Is this what Marco's keeping from me? And if so, why? But also, they were in 'the life'? As in mafia shit...? And I'm Italian? My heart begins to beat erratically in my chest, but I control my breathing as best I can.

"This is all news to me, a—"

Gabriella cuts in, seemingly oblivious to the bombs she's dropping on me as she speaks. "The night they all died was horrific, everyone thought you had been killed in the accident too, but you have a guardian angel. Your parents, your grandparents; Kastellanos thought they'd wiped out the whole Volpe family that night. We all did. But I'm glad they didn't succeed." She smiles at me then, and tears prick my eyes as my whole world implodes.

I should respond, say something, ask questions. I've been preparing myself for answers for so long, and this is *not* what I was expecting. *But how could I ever prepare myself for this?*

I need to speak to Marco.

"This is a lot to take in."

"I know, *bella*. My son should have told you a long time ago, and there is a little more to it, but please go easy on him. All he's ever wanted is you."

Stefano is a fucking genius. I excused myself from Gabriella, clutching little Bruce in my arms because I couldn't bear to put him down, his soft fur soothing me, and I bumped straight into the old Italian man. It's like he knew I needed him—as always, like the freaking ninja he is. Persuading him to give me information on where Marco has gone wasn't as difficult as I'd expected, but—in his words—he hadn't been instructed *not* to tell me, so he didn't see anything wrong with it.

So now I'm driving Marco's Aston Martin down the Grand Central Parkway toward Long Island. I hate driving, but there's no way I was waiting on public transport to go and give my husband an earbashing. Bruce is in the passenger seat, my little mascot for the journey that's going to take me over an hour.

Ugh.

Over an hour of my own thoughts, of wondering what my family was really like. If Mom and Dad left to live the way they did for their own safety somehow. Why we barely saw my grandparents. What the fuck was that party we went to the night they died? When did my grandparents die? How the Hell are the Mancinis' connected to my family? Is Fox my real surname, or is it Volpe? I didn't even know Volpe was a surname, just some random Italian word I've seen tattooed on Marco's ribs. I have a thousand questions and I want my answers from the man with a thousand secrets.

My destination finally comes into view, and if the phrase "creepy vibes" had a picture for definition, this area would be it. The warehouse building looms above me as I pull up outside. I'm not even sure this is the right place, it looks deserted. Hmm. My usual security team, Aly and Justin, aren't with me today, I told them I was going straight to Marco and promised not to make any stops on the way so I wouldn't need them. But now that I'm here, I'm realizing that was probably a bad idea.

Fuck it, there's no one around. I'll just check it out and if he's not here, I'll call him to see exactly where he is. I wanted the element of surprise when confronting him about this, no more time for bullshit excuses, but if I've been led on a wild goose chase by Stefano then I'll go to the man himself.

"You stay here for a minute, Brucey. I'll come back for you when I know he's in there." Ruffling his fur, I kiss his little head before getting out of the car, heading for the warehouse door.

Knocking is for wimps, so I go straight for the handle, pulling the door open wide. Marco is right there as soon as I do and my eyes widen in surprise at his close proximity. He's lucky I didn't throat punch him—thank you, Lina, for showing me how effective that move is.

"We need to—" Before I can finish my sentence, Marco grabs my upper arm, pulling me inside and almost dragging me along. "What the fuck, Marco? Let me go!" He doesn't answer, and it's just fueling my anger toward him. This isn't happening, he isn't controlling this situation. I pull against him, yanking my arm from his grip and planting my feet to the ground. "Will you just stop—" He cuts me off again, bending over and pushing his shoulder into my stomach, lifting me into a fireman's hold. The move winds me a little, and I struggle to get down as he carries me to fuck knows where.

Finally putting me down inside some windowless room, he grabs me by the back of the head, looking me in the eye, and I'm so confused. He looks... scared? Not an expression I've ever seen on him before. My heart stops when I hear shots being fired in the other room, and the reason for Marco's caveman actions suddenly become clear. There's danger here.

"I love you, Tesoro, and I need you to stay safe. Promise me."

My eyes widen at his words. He better not think this is some kind of goodbye.

"I promise. Don't go, Marco. Don't, please stay—" I'm begging him because I need him, suddenly the secrets all seem inconsequential. I'd rather keep Marco for a lifetime than have all the answers I'm seeking. Fuck them. They're no longer important. Marco is.

He kisses me, hard, pouring every ounce of his love into it, his warm breath hovering over my lips as he slowly pulls away.

"I'll be right back."

I'm still in complete shock as he slams the door closed and everything goes quiet, then I try the handle, finding it locked.

"Don't you fucking walk away from me, Marco! Let me the fuck out! Now!" Banging on the solid metal door is doing fuck all apart from making me feel better. It's unmoving. "Marco!"

Nothing.

Pure silence.

Panic is beginning to consume me and I'm getting sick and fucking tired of constantly feeling this way. There are people out there with guns and Marco's behavior scared the shit out of me. Tears prick at my eyes as I scream at the top of my lungs, letting out every ounce of emotion running through my veins. Again and again, I scream, I yell, I smash my fists against the door, determination to get out of here at the top of my mind.

Marco can handle himself, I've seen it, and there's no way Enzo would let him get hurt. I'm not worried for them.

I'm not.

I'm not worried they'll get hurt.

No.

My throat is sore, my face damp from tears, and my whole body shakes with adrenaline. I don't know how long I've been in this dark room, it could be five minutes, it could be fifteen, but when the door finally opens, I lunge for the exit, desperate to see Marco.

It's not him. Instead, a blonde woman is standing there, the same one that was here when I arrived, and she's covered in blood. I push past her into the main space and nearly throw up at the sight before me. There must be at least twenty bodies lying around, some with missing limbs, others with half their face missing, blood, guts and probably brain matter are scattered all over the floor.

"River..."

The woman's voice is soft and she has a British accent, which takes me by surprise, but I have no time to give that my attention right now. I need to find Marco.

"Where is he?" Asking her name or why she's here are secondary questions, unimportant in this moment as I frantically search the room of bodies for him.

"River... they took them."

My heart stops.

My breath completely disappears.

My knees buckle, but I remain standing firm. He's not dead. If someone took him, he has to be alive, which means there is hope.

"Who the fuck are *they*?" I turn to the woman and her face is hard, firm, but I see an ounce of fear there too.

"Ambrosio."

One word and I am seeing red. There's only one Ambrosio I know. Elizabeth. Was our little conversation in the bathroom last night all a big joke to her? Was the little bitch lying through her perfectly white teeth? Hold on... them?

"And who is *them*?"

"Marco and Enzo."

"Fuck."

"Yeah, you got that right. Listen, I'm J. One of Marco's capos. Leader of the Reapers. I know we've never met, but my loyalty to Marco extends to you. What are my orders, boss?" She's so eager to shed blood, I can see it in her eyes.

I can easily identify the emotion because it's currently coursing through my veins. The foreign feeling inside me is only growing bigger with every moment that passes, making itself a home and becoming my sole focus.

"Do you know where they've gone?" I know it's a reach, but she wouldn't be a capo if she wasn't good at her job. She *has* to know something.

I've never been so thankful for my compartmentalization skills and my ability to mask my true feelings.

Before she answers, I hold up a finger, spotting a dark ball of fluff by the exit. My stomach jumps up into my throat as I run over to make sure it's not what I think it is.

It is.

"Aaarrgghh! Those sick fucking bastards!"

I *want* to crumble into a thousand pieces on the blood-covered ground. I *want* to lose all hope and let sadness overwhelm me.

But I *need* to find my husband.

I *need* to find the people who did this.

And I *need* to make sure they pay for it.

Catching a glimpse of the outside, I see the Aston is smashed up through blurry eyes, the passenger door ripped off, and I bend to scoop up the beautiful bundle of fluff who stole my heart. My cheeks are streaked with fat tears and I don't try to stop them. This is all so much, but I'm still standing.

They won't win.

Revenge has never really been in my wheelhouse, but taking the love of my life, killing his mom's dog, making my life a fucking nightmare... someone has to pay.

The moral compass that is my family will understand.

I won't rely on the legal options because they're as useful as tits on a fish, but one way or another...justice will prevail.

Marco once told me he would let the world fall to ashes if it meant saving me and, at the time, I thought it was a lot, but now? Now I get it.

They can all rot in Hell, and I'm going to be the one to put them there.

To be continued in The Forever One

https://geni.us/TheForeverOne

# The Blonde One

Book freakin' five!! A year ago, Brunette and I began this crazy journey of writing together. And it has been amazing. My hubs has deemed her my book wife, and so that is now her name forevermore.

February 2023 will be our one-year publishaversary, and also when we release the finale of The Escort series, but don't despair... we have some new stories planned!

Our fabulous editor, David Michael, didn't quit this time round... yai? :) This book gives you more insight, setting the final pieces in place ready for the last book... just remember... we asked you to trust us, and this is the last cliffhanger of the series we will leave you on.

Over the last couple of months, some readers have surprised us and given us such massive heads as we've seen posts in some of the amazing reader groups recommending and showing off pages from our books. And let me tell ya, these recs and comments and posts we see are like magic to us <3 So, thank you.

P.S... the ending... blame John Wick.

# THE BRUNETTE ONE

It's hard to do this after Blondie, she nails these end-of-the-book sidenotes like a champ but I shall try my best not to fall short.

First off, I want to thank you. Every single one of you has contributed in some way to our happiness. From simply reading our books to rating and reviewing to sharing our graphics on social media to screaming your love for us from the rooftops. Okay, fine, I made that last one up but, hey, hope springs eternal from what I'm told.

A book is never written alone and in our case, it's not even written by just the two of us. There's an entire village behind us pushing us to be the best we can be and I just want to take this time to profess my utter love and respect to you all.

David, our dear editor, may often yell at us for choosing to rip his heart out or piss him off with our shenanigans but

I'm willing to bet that he loves us anyway and would never, truly, quit on us. At least, I hope.

Sam O'Neill, our fierce P.A., makes sure we are on track with our newsletters and street team and I'm not quite sure where we'd be without her so thank you, Sam, for having our backs! If you're an author or P.A. and would like to do a NL swap, feel free to contact her.

Our Betas…Sam and Lydia…we put them through the ringer every time but worse than that is that we giggle when they come out of it completely distraught. Yeah, yeah…evil bitches, we know, we know. Thank you, loves, for being there for us.

Gabri, Gabri, Gabri, where would we be without you and your beautiful language? Let me just say, if Gabri weren't here going through our manuscripts with a fine tooth comb, our Italian would be complete and utter shit. And, well, Marco wasn't having that, was he?

Last but never ever least is Lily/Sloane who makes sure our books look as pretty as humanly possible and we love her for it.

They say you shouldn't judge a book by its cover, but you and I both know that bullshit. We don't just judge them, we spend our hard earned money to have them as trophies on our bookshelves. Well, The Escort series owes its beauty to Bailey Grayson and her witchy ways. Thank you, friend, for putting up with our perfectionism. You're amazing! But none of this would be possible without YOU. The readers, the ones who curl up on a couch and get lost in our words. You'll never understand the utter privilege it is to know our imagination feeds your needs.

Thank YOU for taking a chance on us.

# BOOKS BY N.O. ONE

## Dark Contemporary Romance

**The Escort Series (MF)**

The Rich One ~ https://geni.us/TheRichOne

The Kinky One ~ https://geni.us/TheKinkyOne

The Filthy One ~ https://geni.us/TheFithyOne

The Broken One ~ https://geni.us/TheBrokenOne

The Almost One ~ https://geni.us/TheAlmostOne

The Forever One ~ https://geni.us/TheForeverOne

The Christmas One ~ Prequel to The Escort Series

**KOK (RH)**

Kings of Kink ~ https://geni.us/KingsOfKink

**The Reapers Mafia Crew Duet (MF)**

One Kill ~ https://geni.us/TheReapers1

One Love ~ https://geni.us/TheReapers2

**The Psycho Trilogy – Sons of Khaos (MF)**

Psycho Hate ~ https://geni.us/PsychoHate

Psycho Love ~ https://geni.us/PsychoLove

Psycho Reign ~ https://geni.us/PsychoReign

**A Night To Remember Auction (MF)**

Fatal

**Sons of Khaos – The Standalones**

Bear Hunt (MF) ~ https://geni.us/SOKBearHunt

Meat Grinder (Poly with MF and MM)

**7 Deadly Sins – A Shared World**

Gluttony ~ https://geni.us/SDSGluttony

**Next Door**

The Assassin Next Door

# Dark Paranormal Fantasy Romance

### Society Of Soulkeepers

Hack (MF) ~ Book 1 of The White Horse Duet

Hex (MF) ~ Book 2 of The White Horse Duet

If you'd love to get in touch or find out more about our books, please feel free to stalk us in all the places and join our newsletter.

www.author-no-one.com

Here is our linktree: https://linktr.ee/n.o.one

# BOOKS WE THINK YOU SHOULD READ

# Dark Romance

DATE WITH THE DEVIL (MF) ~
HTTPS://GENI.US/DWTD

# Contemporary

## THE UCC SAGA

DISHEVELED ~ HTTP://AMZN.TO/2ARPBXP
DISARMED ~ HTTP://AMZN.TO/2MYVXNN
DISCARDED ~ HTTPS://AMZN.TO/2VWTRPF
UCC BOXSET ~ HTTPS://AMZN.TO/3LJVEPE

## STANDALONE
THE WISH ~ HTTPS://AMZN.TO/2FTIKQB

# Rom-Com

## THE WOOLF FAMILY SERIES
SCREWED ~ HTTPS://GENI.US/SCREWED
SCREWED UP ~ HTTPS://BIT.LY/3IBFWKB
SCREWED OVER (COMING SOON)

# Supernatural

## SOUL GUARDIANS SERIES
REPRISE ~ HTTPS://BIT.LY/3CT9NPE

## Eva LeNoir
Fun Flirty Romance

# BY LILY WILDHART

**Dark Romance**

**The Saints of Serenity Falls series (RH)**

(You will find crossovers from The Escort series by N.O.
One in the Serenity Falls series by Lily Wildhart, and vice
versa!)

A Burn So Deep ~ https://geni.us/burnaltcover

A Revenge So Sweet ~ https://geni.us/revengealtcover

A Taste Of Forever ~ https://geni.us/tastealtcover

Website & Newsletter: www.author-no-one.com

Facebook: https://geni.us/Facebookauthor

Facebook Group: https://geni.us/FierceReaders

Instagram: https://geni.us/Instagramauthor

Goodreads: https://geni.us/Goodreadsauthor

Bookbub: https://www.bookbub.com/profile/n-o-one

Linkedtree https://linktr.ee/n.o.one